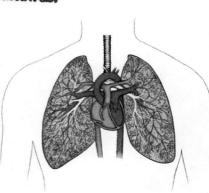

THE
HUMAN
BODY

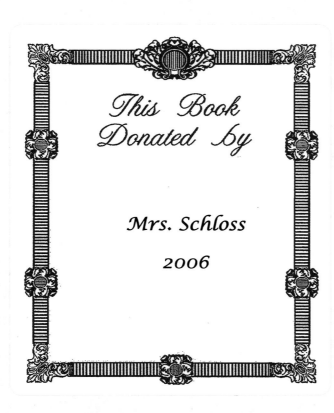

*This Book
Donated by*

Mrs. Schloss

2006

The RANDOM HOUSE
LIBRARY OF KNOWLEDGE™

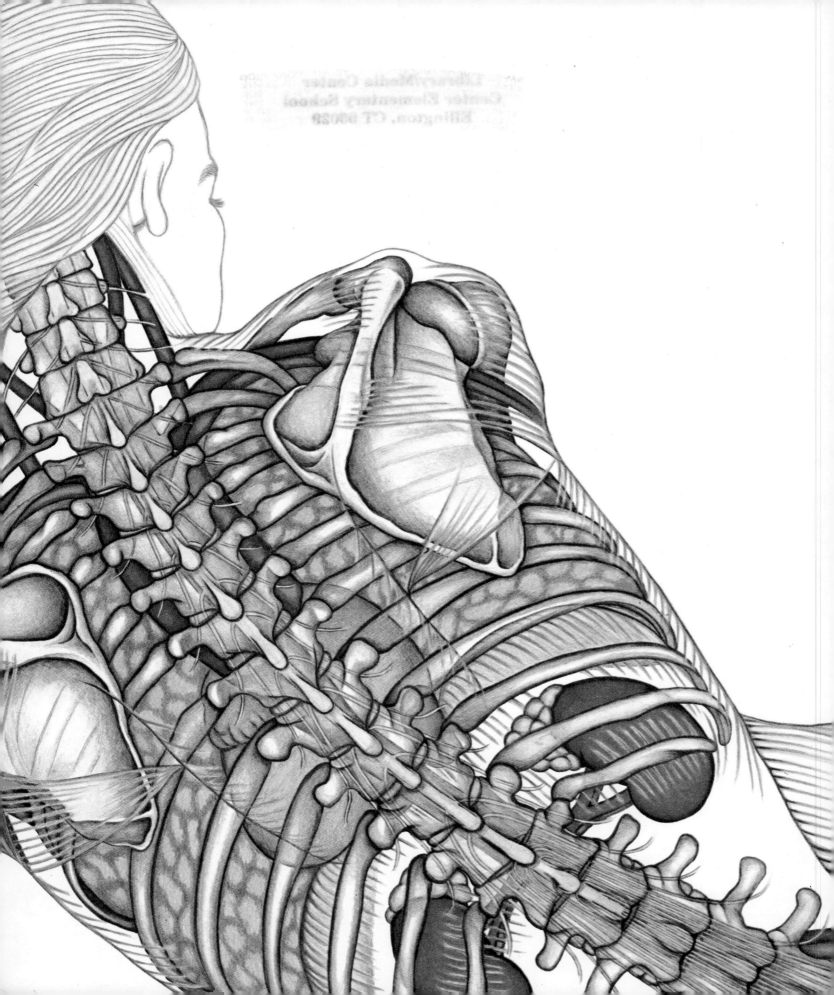

THE HUMAN BODY

BY **Ruth Dowling Bruun**, M.D.

Assistant Professor of Psychiatry,
Cornell University

AND **Bertel Bruun**, M.D.

Assistant Professor of Neurology,
Columbia University

ILLUSTRATED BY **Patricia J. Wynne**

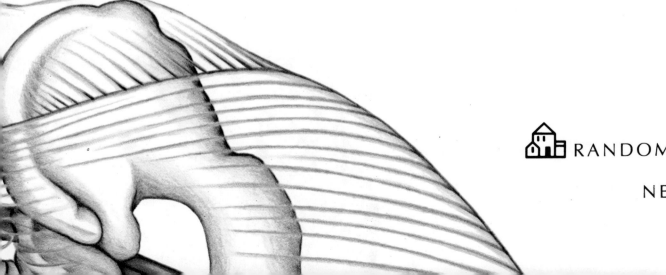

 RANDOM HOUSE

NEW YORK

This book is dedicated to Thomas and Christian

—untiring critics.

More than two years in the making, this book has indeed been a collaborative venture. Patricia Wynne's beautiful and accurate illustrations speak for themselves and attest to her talent and ingenuity. It has been a delight to work with her. Janet Finnie, through her patient expertise, gave invaluable help in making the text comprehensible, yet comprehensive. Without this help, the typographic design by Jos. Trautwein, and the editorial skills of Anne Christensen, the book would not have been possible. Many others gave suggestions and advice freely. We thank them all. For errors that may have occurred, we, however, take full responsibility.

July 1982

Ruth Dowling Bruun, M.D.
Bertel Bruun, M.D.

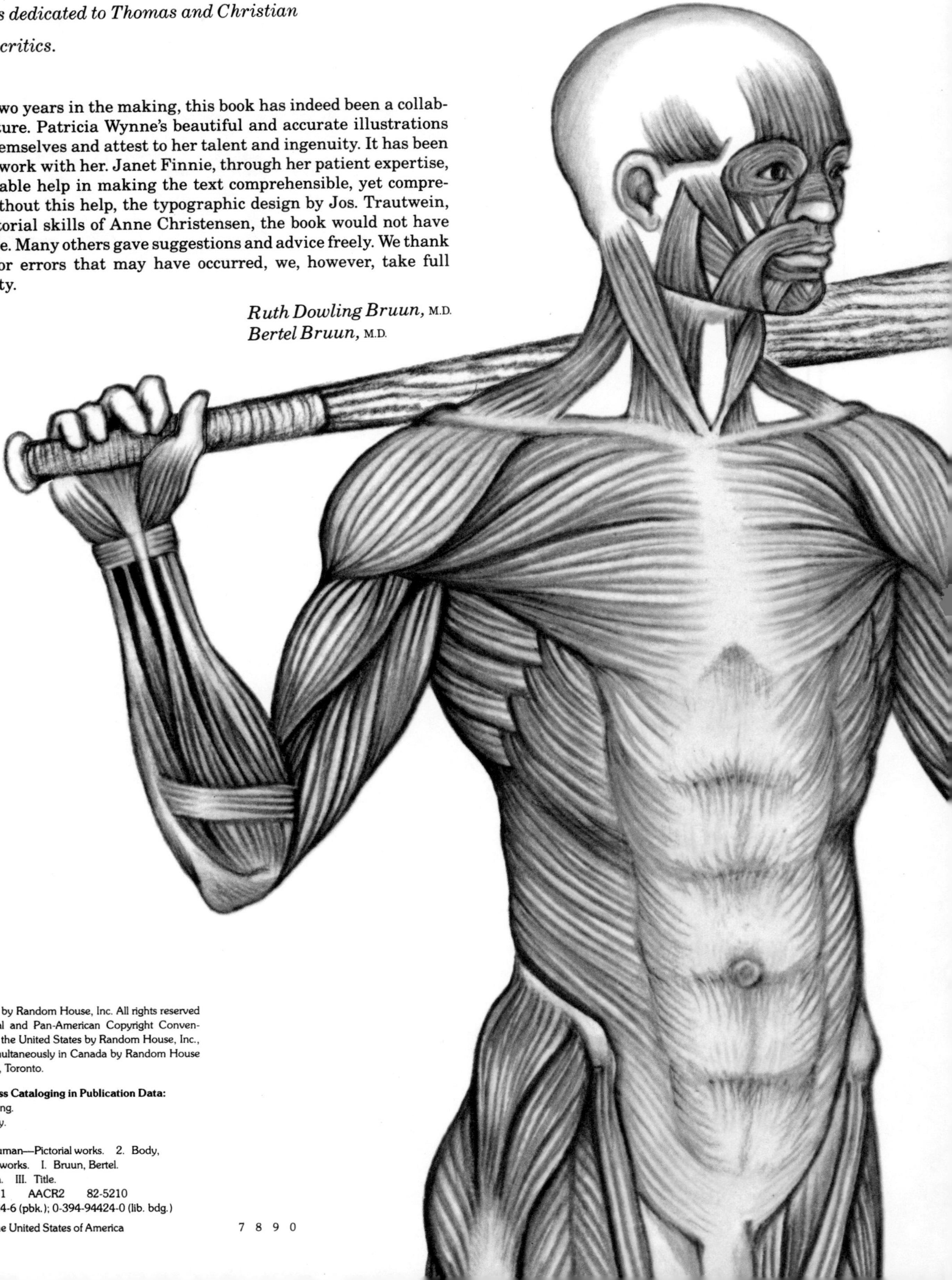

Library of Congress Cataloging in Publication Data:
Bruun, Ruth Dowling.
    The human body.
    Includes index.
    1. Anatomy, Human—Pictorial works. 2. Body, Human—Pictorial works. I. Bruun, Bertel.
II. Wynne, Patricia.   III. Title.
QM25.B85   611   AACR2   82-5210
ISBN: 0-394-84424-6 (pbk.); 0-394-94424-0 (lib. bdg.)

Manufactured in the United States of America   7 8 9 0

CONTENTS

INTRODUCTION

The design of your body is far more sophisticated than that of the most advanced computer.

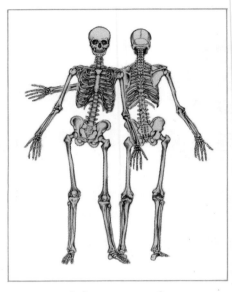

Billions of living cells make up your body. Every one of these cells has special work to do for the sake of your whole body. Similar cells combine into tissues, such as muscle tissue and nerve tissue. Different tissues combine into organs, such as your heart and your lungs. The organs combine into systems, such as your skeletal system and your digestive system. The systems work in groups to serve the needs of the whole organism: you.

The first part of this book, "The Regions of Your Body," illustrates eight areas of the human body, from the head to the feet. Large drawings show your bones, nerves, blood vessels, and many other organs packed neatly together.

The second part, "The Systems of Your Body," explains each major system as a whole, showing how organs and tissues and cells cooperate to carry out the work of the system.

Most of the organs shown and named in "The Regions of Your Body" are shown, named, and discussed under "The Systems of Your Body." The index can often lead to additional information about specific organs.

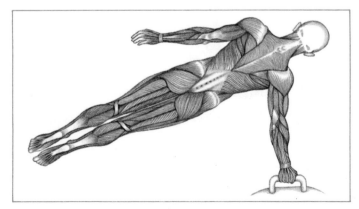

One of the chief purposes of this book is to help the reader become more familiar with the interior of his or her own body. Human bodies vary a little from one person to the next, not only in the visible aspects of size and shape but also in the placement of internal organs. However, human bodies follow a general pattern, which is shown, with variations, throughout this book.

Specific colors are used throughout the book for quick identification of important organs. On page 8 is a color key for organs.

A body organ is, of course, three-dimensional. To help the reader visualize body parts as solid objects, the artist has shown many of them from more than one angle. For example, the protective pelvis is shown from the front, the back, and the side. The elbow is pictured throughout the book from five different angles.

All parts of the human body have technical names (usually from Latin or Greek), and some have common names as well. The common names are often used in this book. Both versions appear in the detailed index. You will find many page references listed for

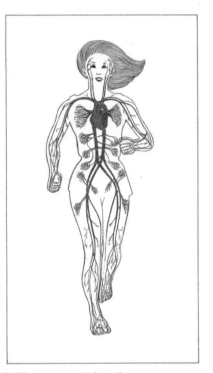

some parts of the body. For instance, the heart is mentioned and illustrated in the circulatory, muscular, and respiratory chapters.

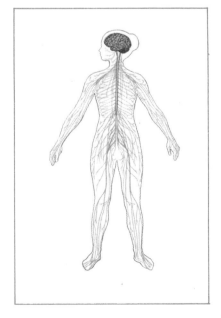

No part of the human body works in isolation. Each does its task tirelessly, day and night, supported and aided by all the other organs.

To understand how the human body works, we must examine its systems one at a time. To understand the beauty and wonder of the human body, we must examine it as a whole. This book attempts to do both.

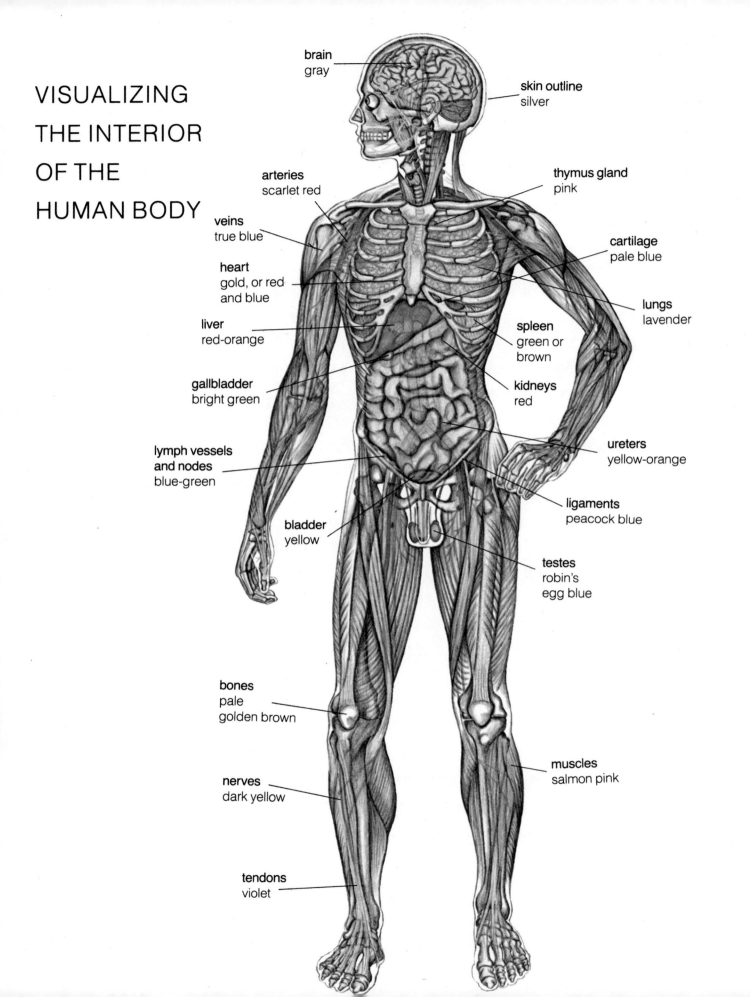

VISUALIZING
THE INTERIOR
OF THE
HUMAN BODY

brain
gray

skin outline
silver

arteries
scarlet red

thymus gland
pink

veins
true blue

cartilage
pale blue

heart
gold, or red
and blue

lungs
lavender

liver
red-orange

spleen
green or
brown

gallbladder
bright green

kidneys
red

lymph vessels
and nodes
blue-green

ureters
yellow-orange

ligaments
peacock blue

bladder
yellow

testes
robin's
egg blue

bones
pale
golden brown

muscles
salmon pink

nerves
dark yellow

tendons
violet

The Regions of
Your Body

THE FOLLOWING 16 PAGES are a visual guide to the internal design of your body.

Two large drawings show the head and neck, from the front and in profile. Four large drawings show different areas of the torso, from the bottom of the neck to the top of your legs. Other large drawings show the arms, legs, hands, and feet.

Each large drawing shows the organs of one area and their relationships to each other. For example, your heart, which works closely with your lungs, fits between them. Both your heart and your lungs are protected by the bony cage formed by your spine, ribs, and breastbone. Your spine also protects the spinal cord and nerves running through your vertebrae, as well as the major blood vessels close by.

Because your body has many parts, one in front of the other, you could never see them all in one picture. Therefore, some parts are shown partially transparent in this book to give you a better view of the body.

For example, the stomach sometimes appears transparent in order to show the pancreas behind it. The breastbone sometimes appears transparent in order to show the trachea (windpipe) behind it.

Muscles are often shown transparent in order to show bones or other structures beneath them. In other cases, surface muscles are omitted entirely to allow you to see interior organs. (Drawings of your muscular system appear later in this book.)

Key drawings accompany each large illustration. They clarify and name the organs and systems in the main illustration. In some cases a key drawing shows completely an organ that is partially concealed in the large illustration.

Readers can use "The Regions of Your Body" in more than one way. Someone interested in a specific organ, such as the brain or the liver, can see where it is located, what other organs are nearby, and the relationships of size and shape. For someone interested in a major area, such as the back, the large drawing and its key drawings will show the bones, muscles, and nerves of this area, as well as the organs just inside the spine.

In "The Regions of Your Body," you can visualize the interior of your body more clearly than you could visualize it from a whole series of X rays.

Head and Neck

Your head contains your brain, which is the largest part of your central nervous system. Some of your sensory organs are located in your head: your eyes, ears, taste buds, and organs of smell.

Your head contains the mouth and nose, openings for receiving the food, water, and oxygen needed by your digestive and respiratory systems. Your skeletal system provides strong, interlocking bones to protect your delicate brain.

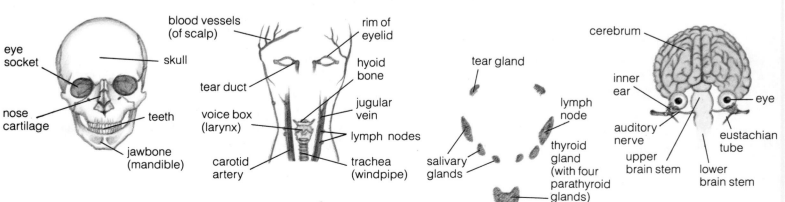

eye socket

skull

blood vessels (of scalp)

rim of eyelid

cerebrum

nose cartilage

tear duct

teeth

hyoid bone

tear gland

inner ear

eye

jawbone (mandible)

voice box (larynx)

jugular vein

lymph node

auditory nerve

eustachian tube

carotid artery

lymph nodes

trachea (windpipe)

salivary glands

thyroid gland (with four parathyroid glands)

upper brain stem

lower brain stem

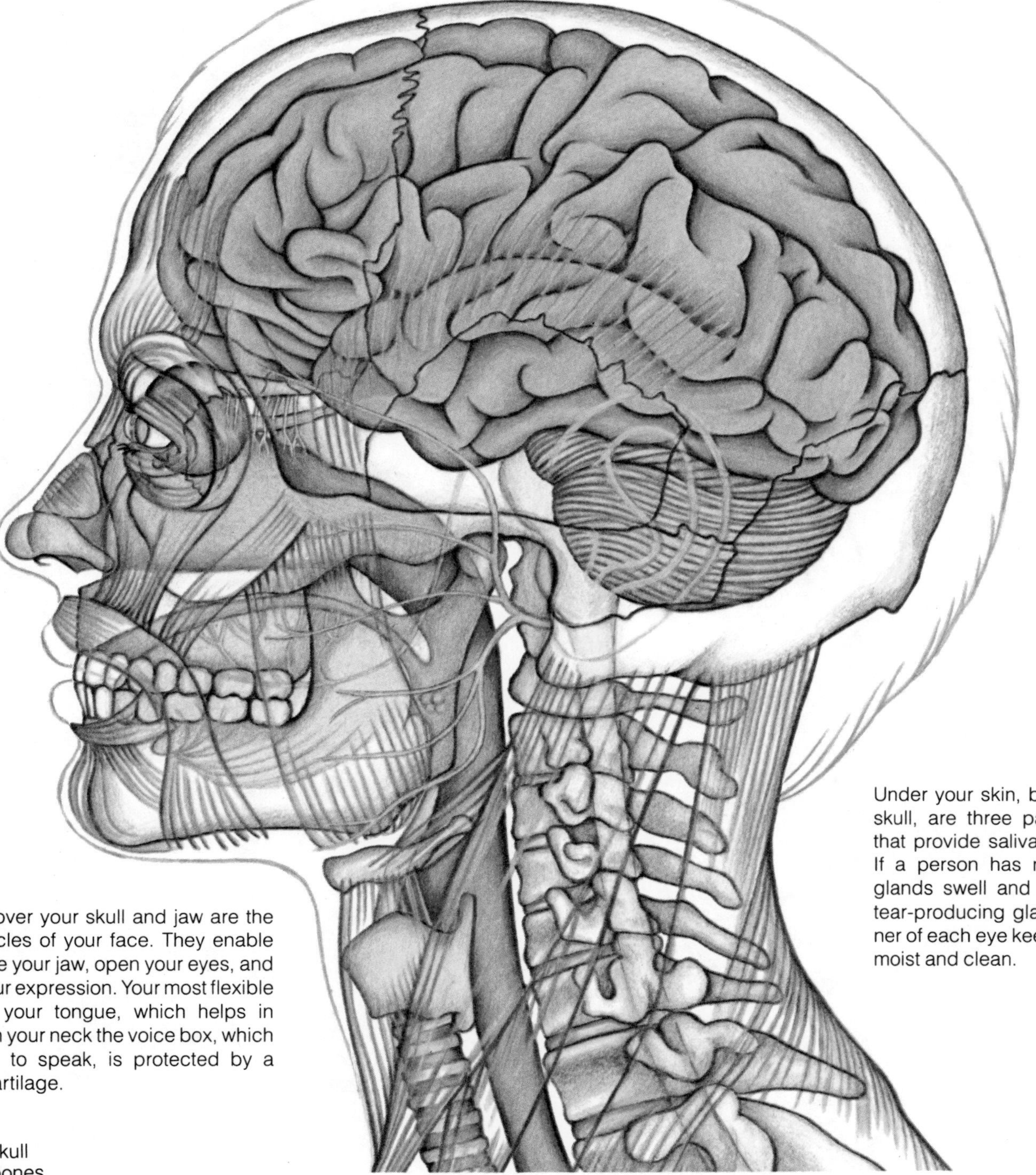

Stretched over your skull and jaw are the many muscles of your face. They enable you to move your jaw, open your eyes, and change your expression. Your most flexible muscle is your tongue, which helps in chewing. In your neck the voice box, which allows you to speak, is protected by a shield of cartilage.

Under your skin, but outside the skull, are three pairs of glands that provide saliva for digestion. If a person has mumps, these glands swell and hurt. The tiny tear-producing gland in the corner of each eye keeps the cornea moist and clean.

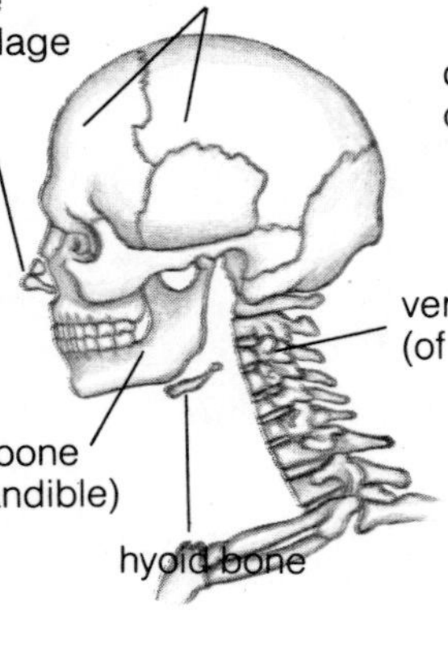

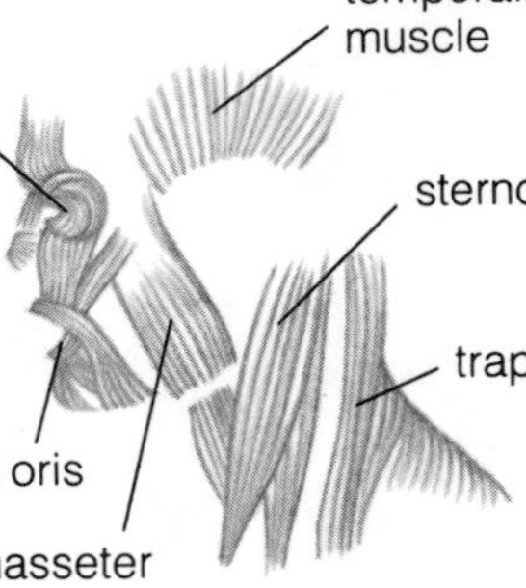

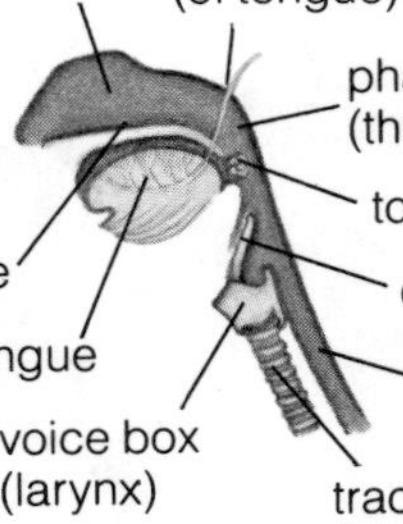

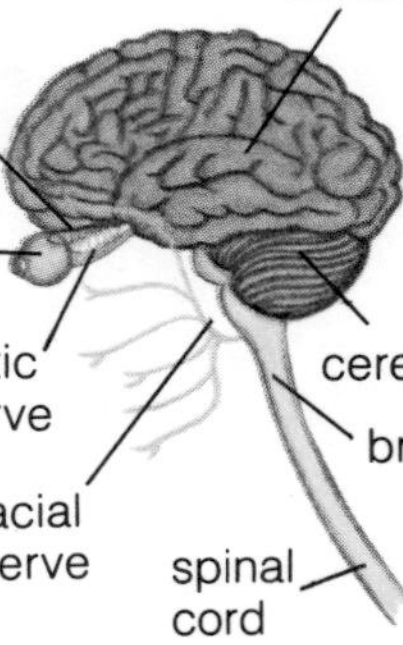

nose cartilage

skull bones

orbicularis oculi

temporalis muscle

nasal cavity

sensory nerve (of tongue)

olfactory bulb

cerebrum

vertebrae (of neck)

sternomastoid

pharynx (throat)

eye

tonsils

palate

jawbone (mandible)

orbicularis oris

trapezius

tongue

epiglottis

optic nerve

cerebellum

voice box (larynx)

esophagus

facial nerve

brain stem

hyoid bone

masseter

trachea (windpipe)

spinal cord

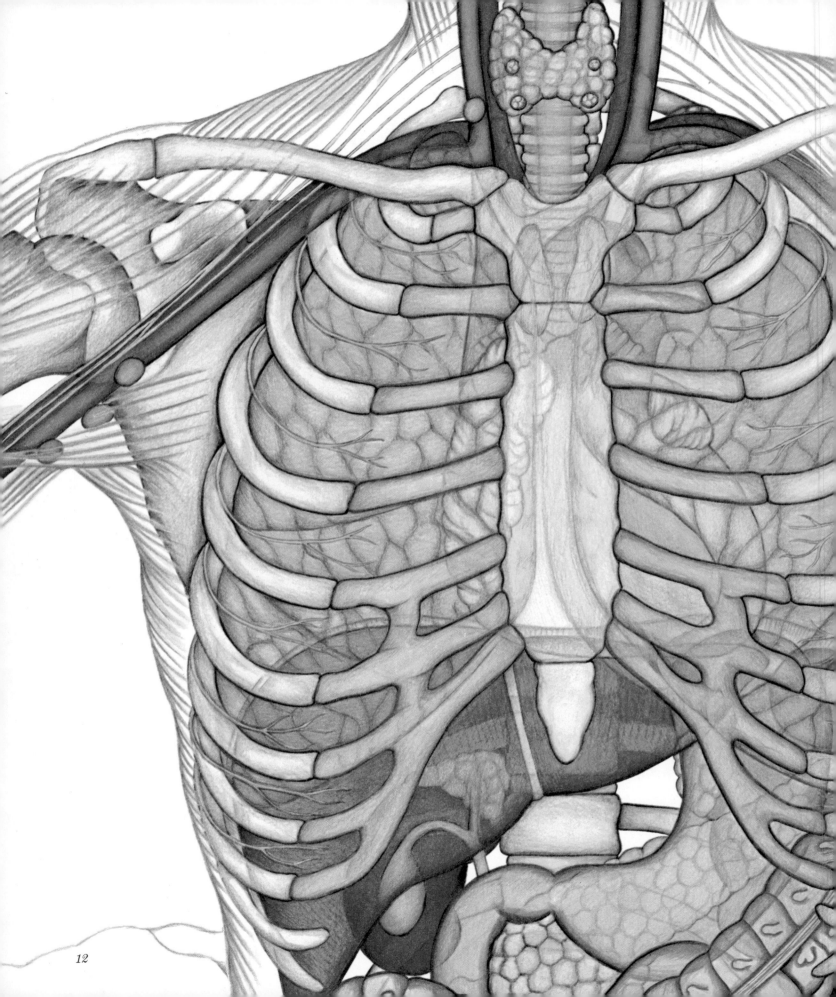

Upper Torso

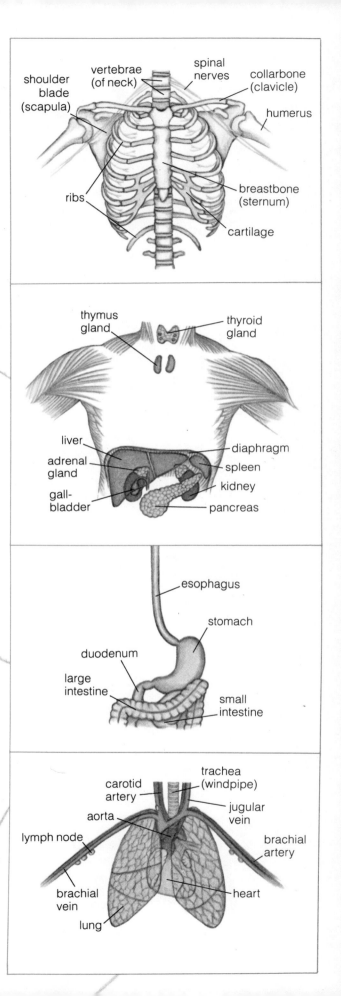

shoulder
blade
(scapula)

vertebrae
(of neck)

spinal
nerves

collarbone
(clavicle)

humerus

ribs

breastbone
(sternum)

cartilage

thymus
gland

thyroid
gland

liver

diaphragm

adrenal
gland

spleen

gall-
bladder

kidney

pancreas

esophagus

stomach

duodenum

large
intestine

small
intestine

trachea
(windpipe)

carotid
artery

jugular
vein

aorta

lymph node

brachial
artery

brachial
vein

heart

lung

Your diaphragm, the strong sheet of muscle that controls your breathing, divides your torso into two cavities of unequal size: the chest cavity (thorax) above the diaphragm, and the larger abdomen below it. This drawing shows all of the chest cavity and the upper part of the abdomen.

Almost filling the chest cavity are your lungs, with the heart between them. These are the chief organs of your respiratory and circulatory systems. The heart and lungs are protected by several parts of your skeletal system: your spine, breastbone, collarbones, and ribs.

Through holes in your diaphragm pass the major blood vessels on their way to and from the lower body. Through another hole the esophagus carries food to your stomach.

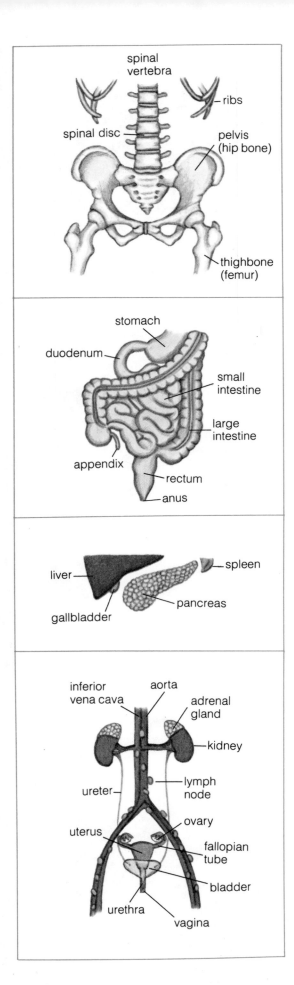

Lower Torso: Female

Your abdominal cavity extends from your diaphragm (pages 12–13) to the bottom of your pelvis. The chief organs and glands of your digestive system are in your abdomen: the stomach, intestines, liver, gallbladder, and pancreas. Blood vessels carry blood through your kidneys for removal of wastes. The kidneys are the chief organs of the urinary system. Two tubes, the ureters, pass urine from the kidneys to the bladder. Below the kidneys, the major blood vessels divide in order to serve your right and left legs.

Many of the body's hormones are produced in the abdomen. The adrenal glands (on top of the kidneys) and the female ovaries are ductless glands of the endocrine system. The pancreas provides the hormone insulin.

An organ of the immune system, the spleen, is located close to the pancreas. (The complete spleen is shown on page 13.) The spleen also helps in the production of blood cells.

The female organs of reproduction are the ovaries, fallopian tubes, uterus, and vagina. They are surrounded by the heavy bone of the pelvis. Because the pelvis has movable joints with the spine and the thighbone, you can bend at the waist and hips.

Except for the organs of reproduction and the wider shape of the pelvis, the interior structure of the female abdomen is much the same as that of the male abdomen (page 17).

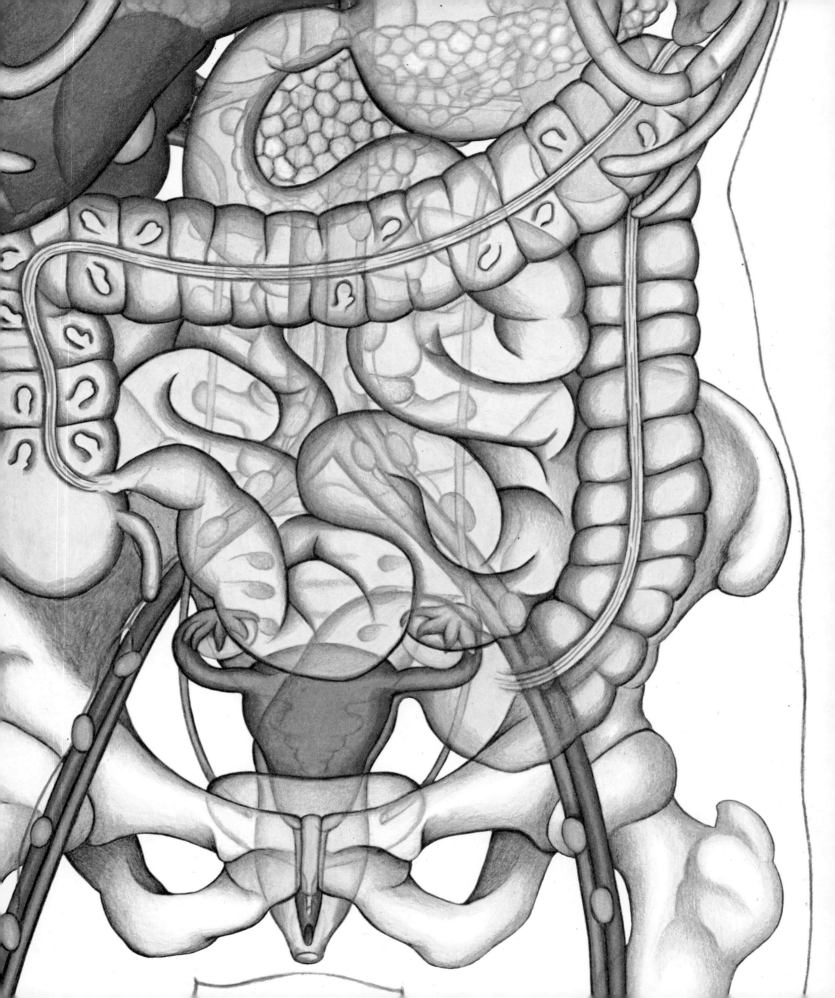

Lower Torso: Male

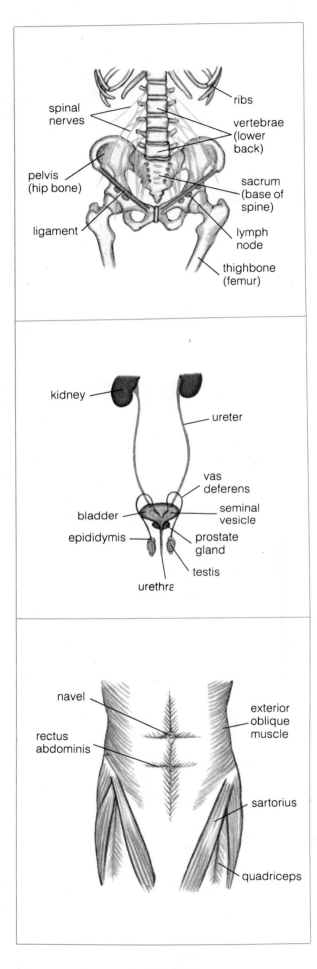

spinal nerves

ribs

vertebrae (lower back)

pelvis (hip bone)

sacrum (base of spine)

ligament

lymph node

thighbone (femur)

kidney

ureter

vas deferens

seminal vesicle

bladder

epididymis

prostate gland

testis

urethra

navel

exterior oblique muscle

rectus abdominis

sartorius

quadriceps

Your spine is composed of many small bones called vertebrae. Emerging from the protection of the vertebrae are your spinal nerves. Shown here are the lower spinal nerves, which control and receive information from your legs, feet, and reproductive organs. The male urethra, which is longer than the female urethra, opens at the end of the penis. In other respects, the male urinary system is the same as the female urinary system (pages 14–15). Some male reproductive organs are sheltered behind the pelvis: the vas deferens, seminal vesicles, prostate gland, and part of the urethra. Other male reproductive organs are outside the pelvis: the testes, epididymis, and penis.

The male abdomen houses the digestive organs, which are like the female digestive organs (pages 14–15). Strong muscles tightly cover the abdomen, supporting your internal organs and wrapping around the body to give strength to your back. Across the sides of the pelvis stretch two thick ligaments, which help the muscular system to hold your intestines in place. Along these ligaments lie a number of lymph nodes.

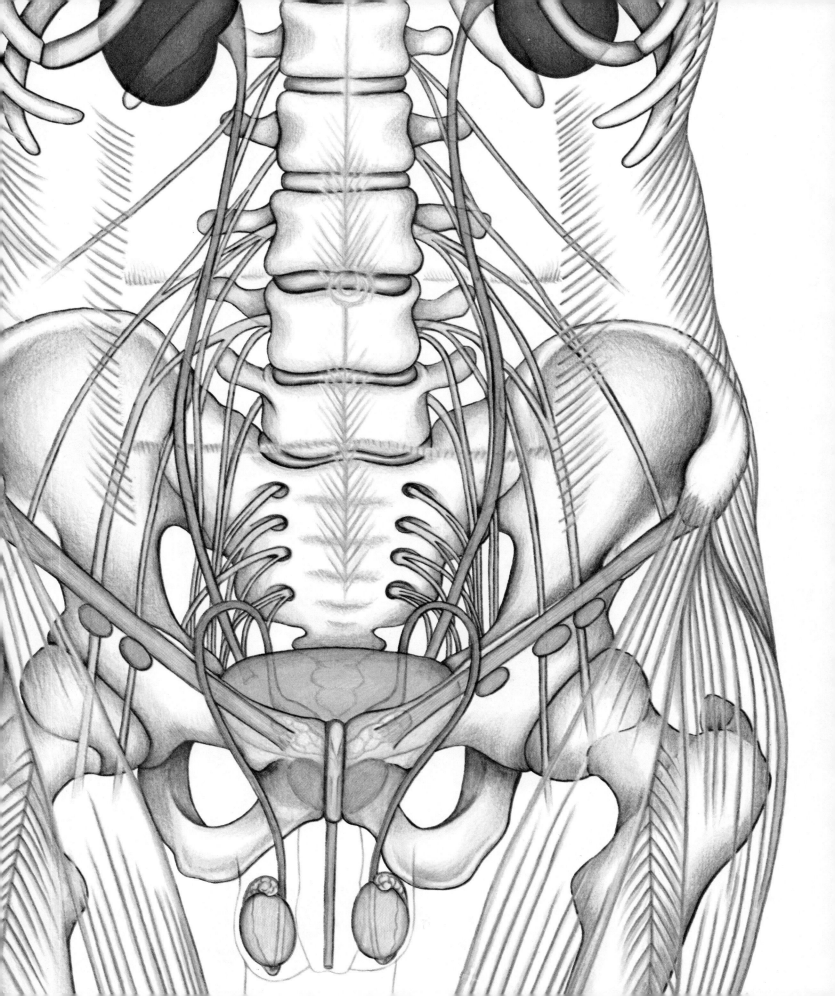

The Back

Your body is flexible enough to twist and bend because your spine contains separate small bones, or vertebrae. Nestled close to the spine are your kidneys, with the adrenal glands on top of them. Your spinal column runs through holes in the vertebrae, and the spinal nerves branch out from the column. Your back muscles bend and straighten your body, support your chest, and give extra power to your arms.

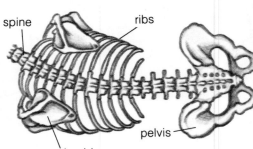

spine

ribs

shoulder blade (scapula)

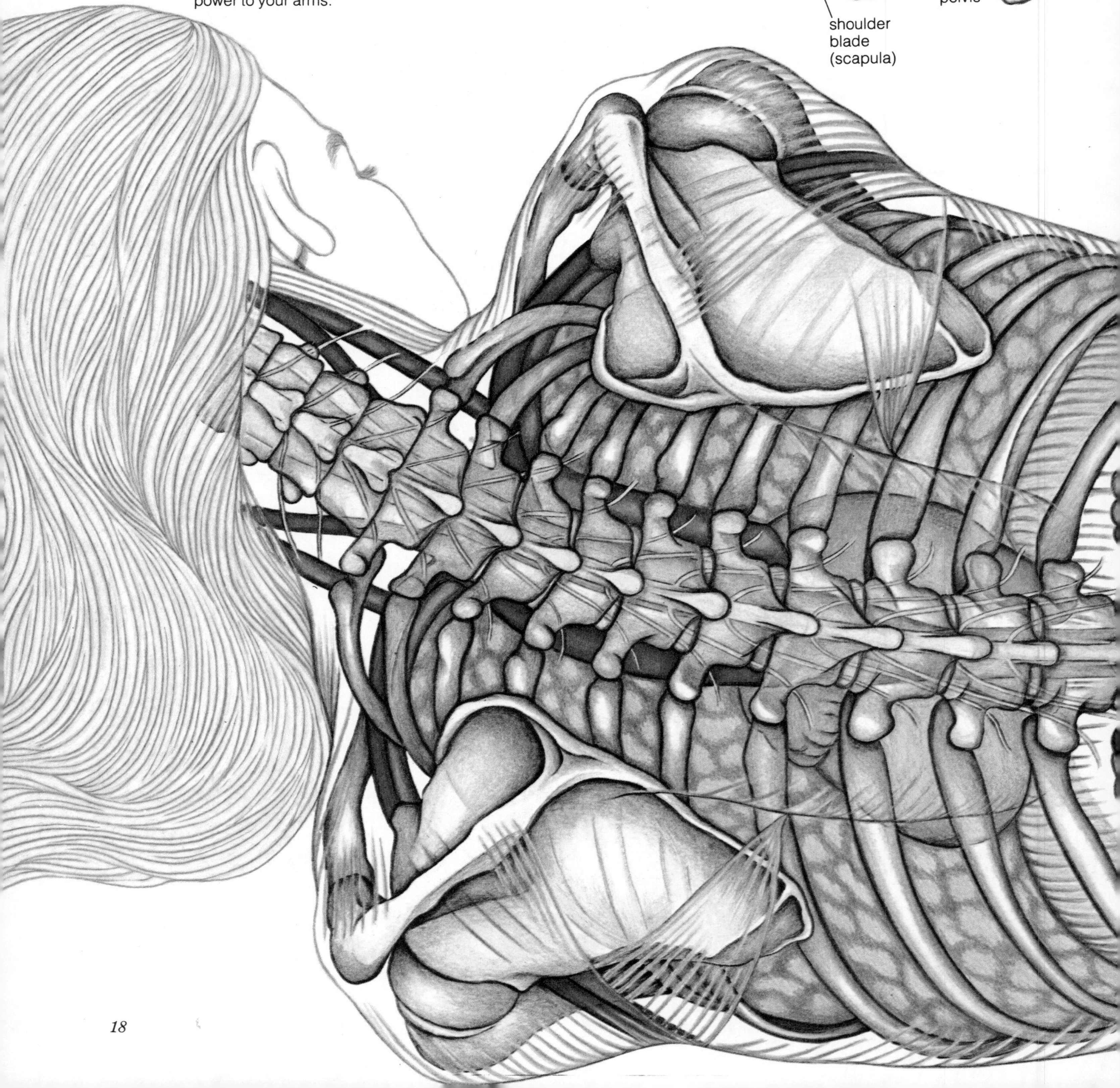

pelvis

18

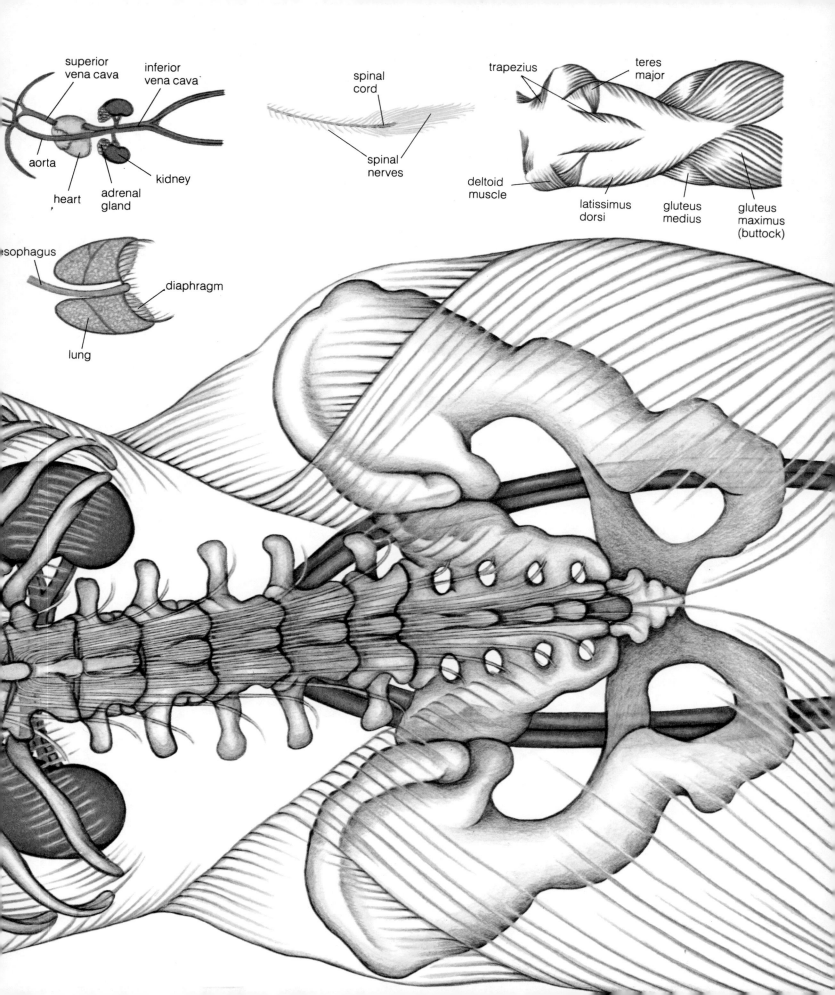

superior
vena cava

inferior
vena cava

aorta

heart

adrenal
gland

kidney

spinal
cord

spinal
nerves

trapezius

teres
major

deltoid
muscle

latissimus
dorsi

gluteus
medius

gluteus
maximus
(buttock)

esophagus

diaphragm

lung

The Arms

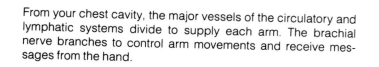

From your chest cavity, the major vessels of the circulatory and lymphatic systems divide to supply each arm. The brachial nerve branches to control arm movements and receive messages from the hand.

Although some bones (skull, ribs, pelvis) chiefly protect other organs, the bones of the arms and legs are chiefly for leverage. The arm, which manipulates the hand, is much more flexible than the leg. The arm muscles, aided by the shoulder muscles, provide for both delicate and forceful movements. At your elbow, the long bone of your upper arm (the humerus) joins the two long bones of your lower arm, the radius and ulna. If you hold your wrist at the sides, you will feel the end of the radius on the thumb side, and the end of the ulna on the little-finger side. You can feel the head of the ulna as the bony part of your elbow. Your elbow joint not only bends but swivels to twist your hand.

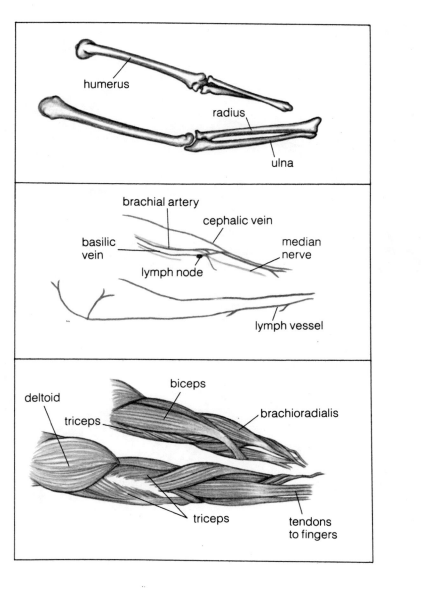

humerus

radius

ulna

brachial artery

cephalic vein

basilic vein

median nerve

lymph node

lymph vessel

deltoid

biceps

triceps

brachioradialis

triceps

tendons to fingers

The Legs

Because your legs support the weight of your whole body, they are much stronger and more stable than your arms. Your legs swing from your hips, the ball-and-socket joints in your pelvis. Your thighbone joins the two long bones of your lower leg, the tibia and fibula, at your knee. If you hold your ankle at the sides, you will feel the end of the tibia on the big-toe side, and the end of the fibula on the little-toe side. Protecting the hinge joint at the knee are the kneecap bone, a pad of fat (shown in yellow), and cushioning sacs called bursae.

The leg has fewer muscles than the arm because the leg does little rotation, but leg muscles are stronger than arm muscles. For example, your two buttock muscles, attached to the thighbone and pelvis, can pull your body upright from a sitting to a standing position.

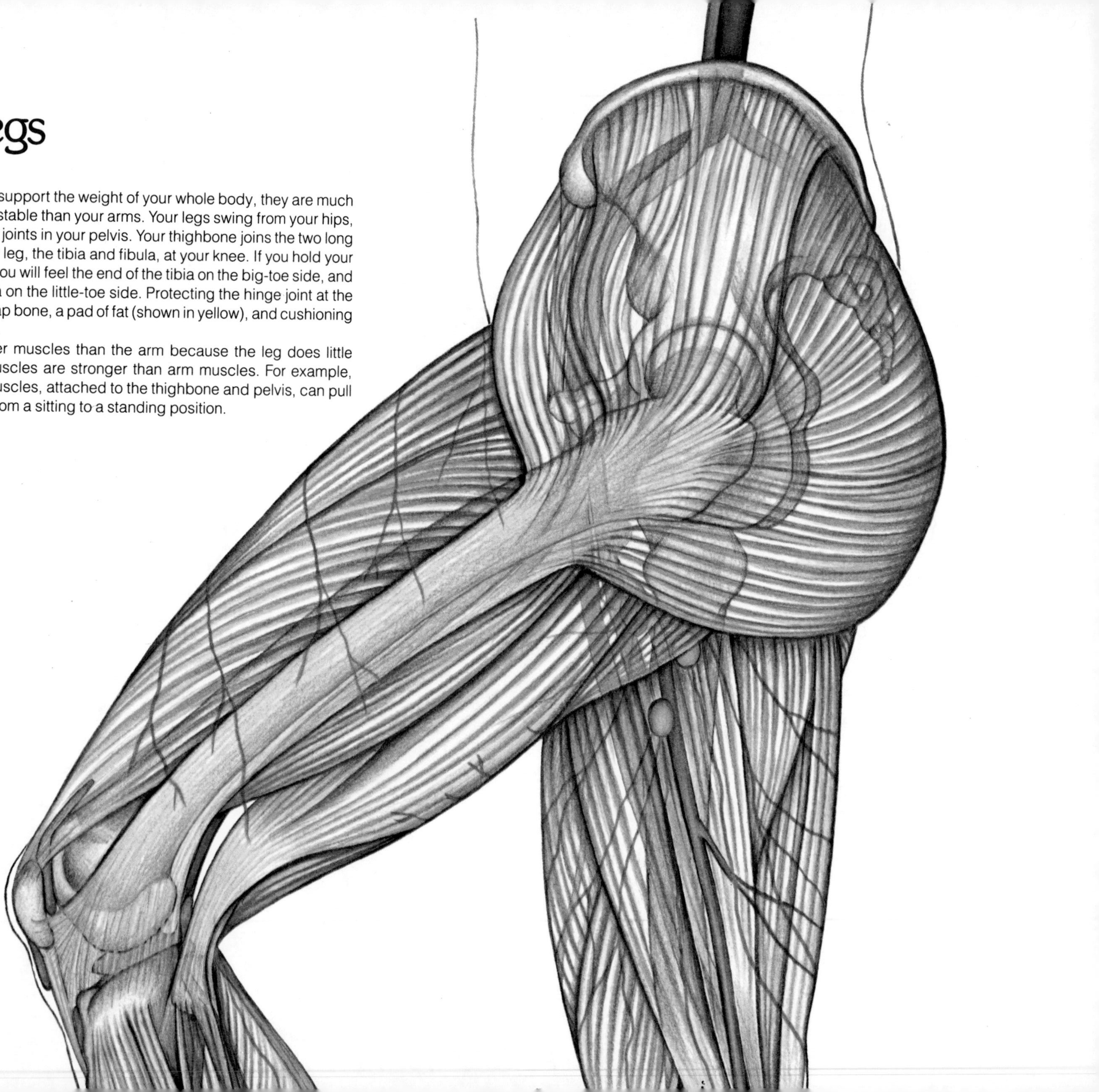

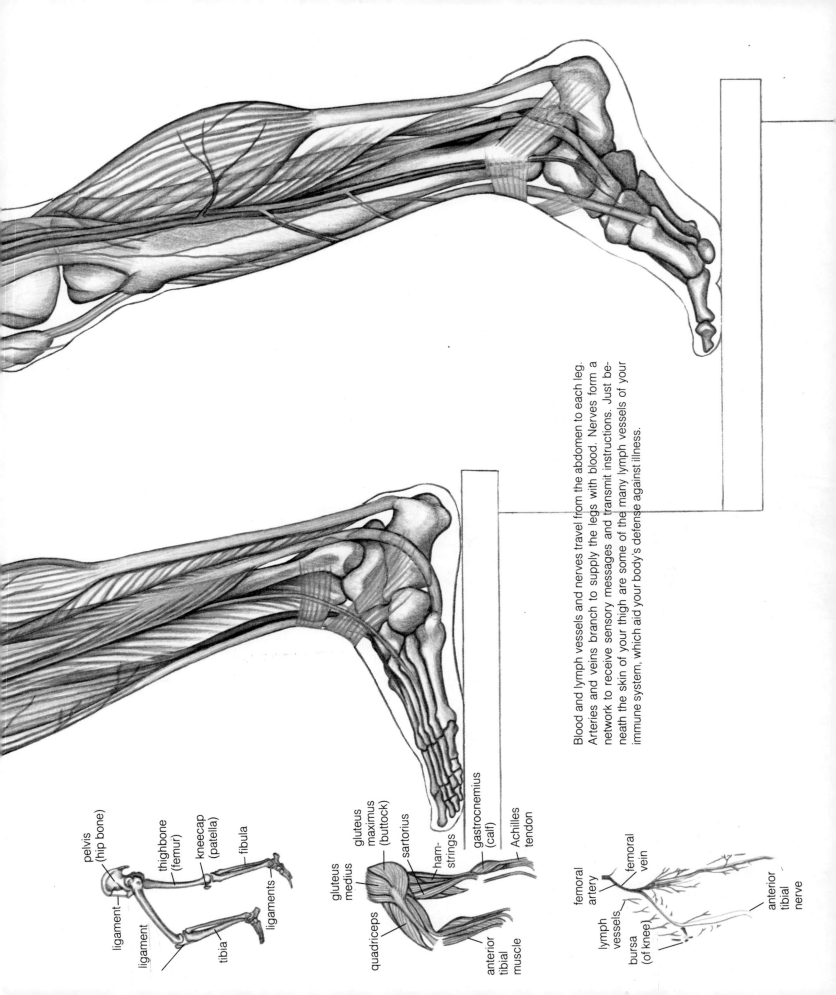

Blood and lymph vessels and nerves travel from the abdomen to each leg. Arteries and veins branch to supply the legs with blood. Nerves form a network to receive sensory messages and transmit instructions. Just beneath the skin of your thigh are some of the many lymph vessels of your immune system, which aid your body's defense against illness.

pelvis (hip bone)
thighbone (femur)
kneecap (patella)
fibula
ligaments
ligament
ligament
tibia

gluteus medius
gluteus maximus (buttock)
sartorius
hamstrings
gastrocnemius (calf)
Achilles tendon
quadriceps
anterior tibial muscle

femoral artery
femoral vein
lymph vessels
bursa (of knee)
anterior tibial nerve

Hands and Feet

The bones of your hand and foot are similar, though somewhat different in size and shape. Your thumb and your big toe have two bones each, while your other fingers and toes have three bones each. A side view of the foot, showing the heel bone, appears on page 23.

The small muscles of the hands and feet are controlled chiefly by tendons from the muscles of the arms and legs. Tendons to your fingers and toes are wrapped in fluid-filled sacs (bursae), helping them slide smoothly when you move a hand or foot.

Your hand is beautifully designed for fine movements and great dexterity. You can move your thumb across your palm to provide a firm grip. Because of this unique feature, human beings can use tools efficiently. A strong ligament around your wrist protects the nerves, tendons, and blood vessels on their way to your fingers. Your fingertips, with a large number of nerve endings, are among the most sensitive parts of your body.

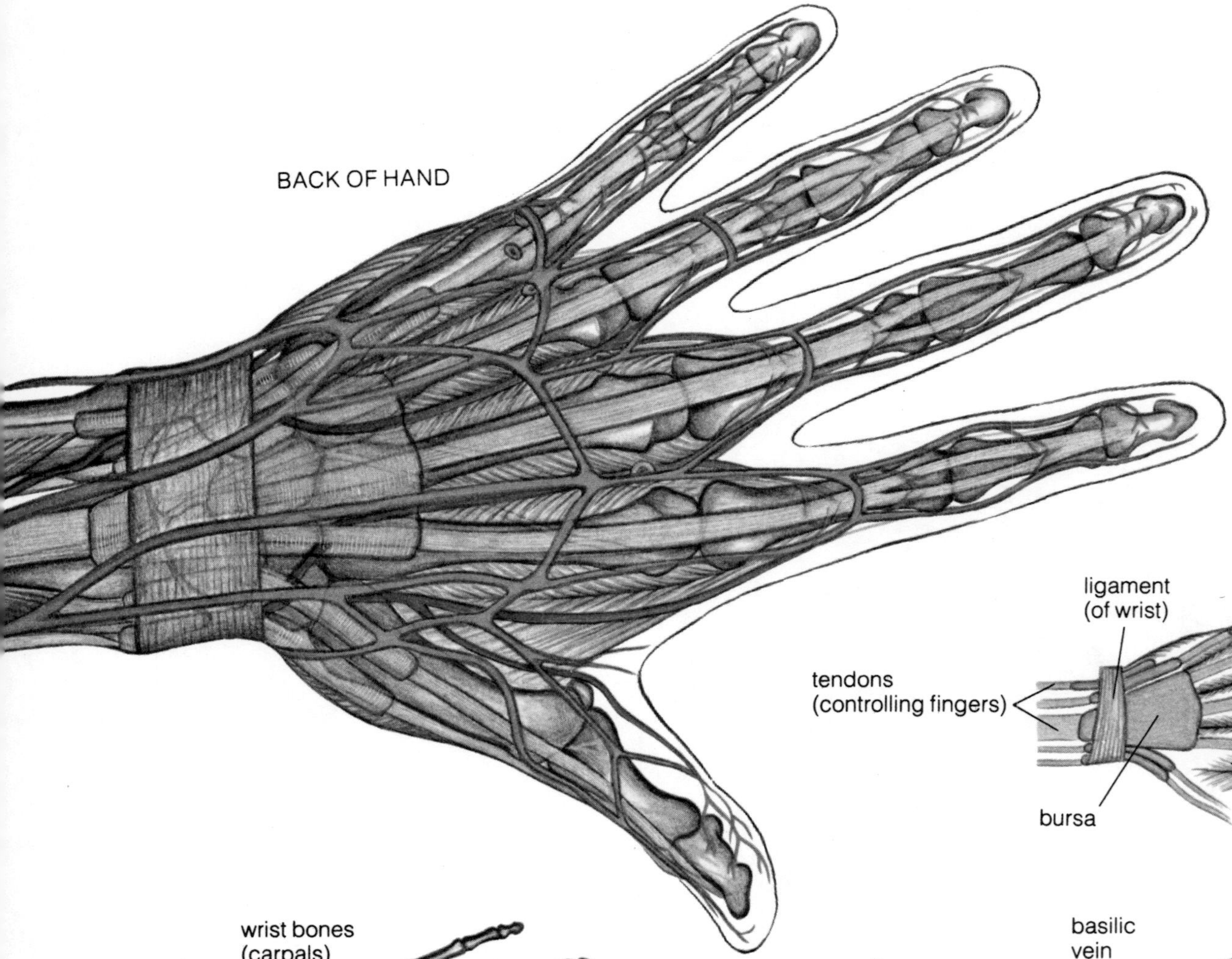

BACK OF HAND

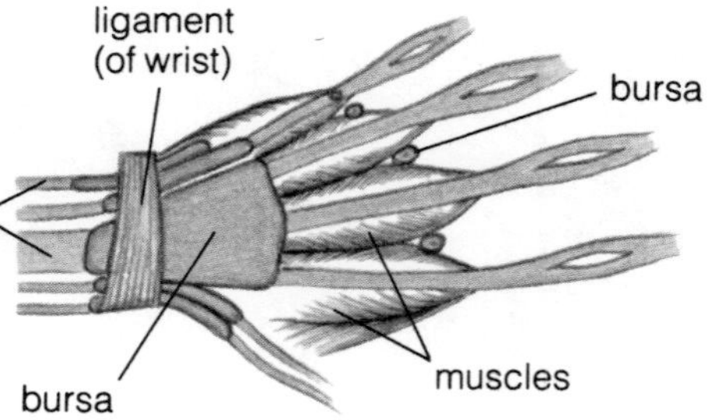

ligament (of wrist)

bursa

tendons (controlling fingers)

bursa

muscles

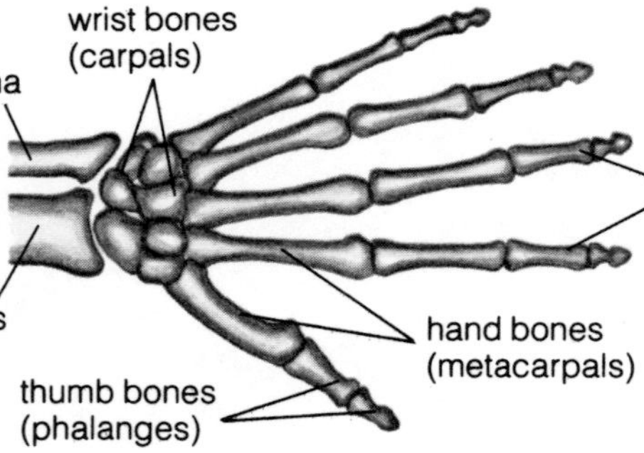

wrist bones (carpals)

ulna

finger bones (phalanges)

radius

hand bones (metacarpals)

thumb bones (phalanges)

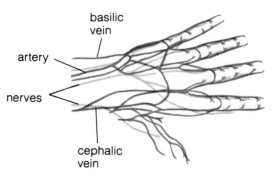

basilic vein

artery

nerves

cephalic vein

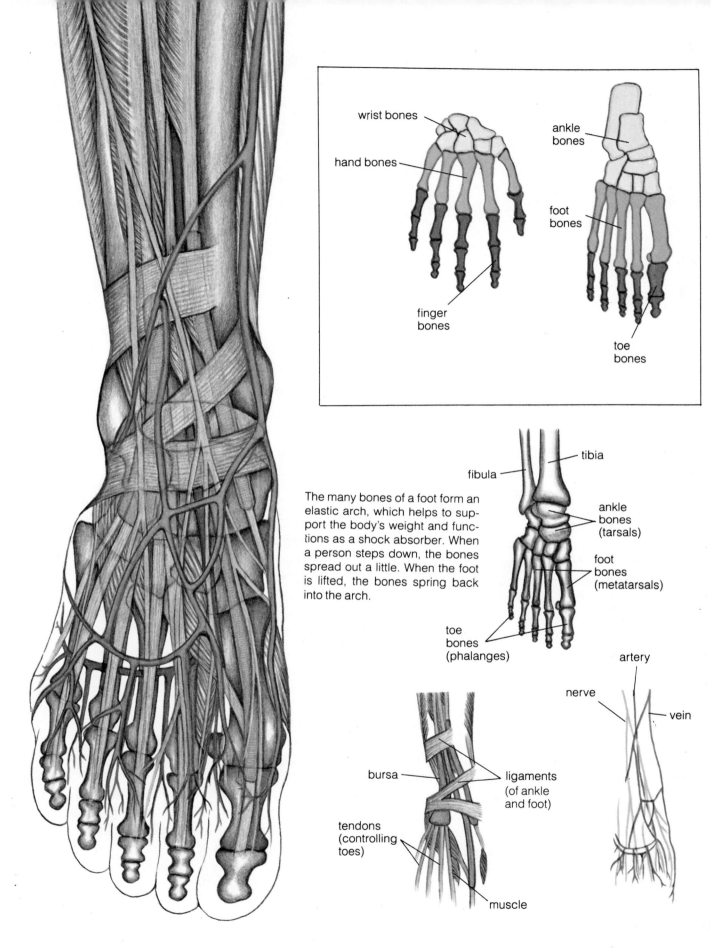

wrist bones

hand bones

finger bones

ankle bones

foot bones

toe bones

fibula

tibia

ankle bones (tarsals)

foot bones (metatarsals)

toe bones (phalanges)

The many bones of a foot form an elastic arch, which helps to support the body's weight and functions as a shock absorber. When a person steps down, the bones spread out a little. When the foot is lifted, the bones spring back into the arch.

artery

nerve

vein

bursa

ligaments (of ankle and foot)

tendons (controlling toes)

muscle

The Systems of Your Body

THE SYSTEMS OF YOUR body work in groups to serve you in important ways. Your skeletal and muscular systems provide support and allow you to move. You need your bones and muscles to get from one place to another, to curl up to sleep, to lift food to your mouth, and to read this book.

Several systems cooperate to provide your body with energy. Your digestive system turns your food into the fuel you need for energy and into the raw materials you need for growth and the repair of your cells. Your respiratory system supplies oxygen to release energy from the fuel. Your circulatory system carries the fuel and raw materials and oxygen to all parts of your body. Your urinary system cooperates with these systems in removing waste materials from your body.

How can the billions of cells in your body work so smoothly together? Several systems are responsible for coordination and control. Your sensory systems report to your brain about what is happening in and around you. The brain is the chief organ of your nervous system, which sends instructions to your muscles, glands, and other organs. Your endocrine system sends hormones through your bloodstream to deliver instructions to many organs.

Finally, the reproductive system allows the crea-tion of a new human being, who is both like and unlike each of the two parents.

Each system of the human body consists of the organs that cooperate to carry out the tasks of the system. For example, the organs of your skeletal system include your bones and ligaments. The organs of your nervous system are your brain, spinal cord, and nerves. The organs of your digestive system include your teeth and tongue, your esophagus and stomach, your small and large intestines and your liver and pancreas.

Each organ consists of one or more kinds of tissue. In your stomach, for example, one kind of tissue provides muscles to churn your food and then move it along to your intestines. A second kind of tissue provides a soft lining that produces digestive juices. A third kind of tissue forms a protective covering over your whole stomach.

Tissues consist of large numbers of similar cells. The cell is the basic unit of life. The cells in your body take many forms, depending largely on their special-ized work, but all living cells are similar in many ways.

"The Systems of Your Body" begins with a discus-sion of the cells and tissues that make up your organs and systems. Later chapters explain and illustrate the workings of the major systems of your body.

SYSTEMS FOR STANDING AND MOVING

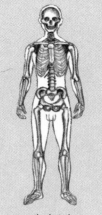 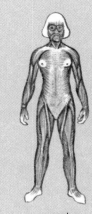

skeletal   muscular

SYSTEMS FOR ENERGY
(AND WASTE DISPOSAL)

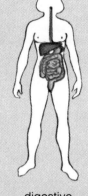 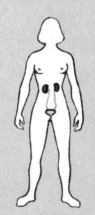

digestive   respiratory   circulatory   urinary

SYSTEMS FOR COORDINATION AND CONTROL

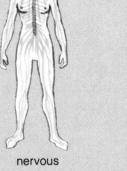 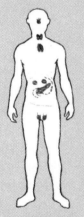

nervous   sensory   endocrine

SYSTEMS FOR PRODUCING NEW LIFE

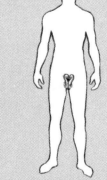 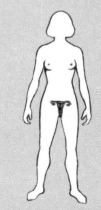

reproductive (male)   reproductive (female)

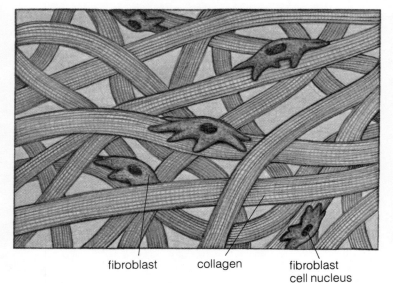

fibroblast   collagen   fibroblast
                          cell nucleus

Connective tissue is your body's packing material. It also connects bones with muscles and with other bones.

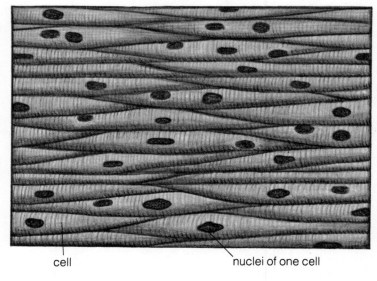

cell   nuclei of one cell

Muscle tissue consists of cells that can contract, producing all your body's external and internal movements.

Tissues and Cells

THE ORGANS OF your body are made of different kinds of tissues — groups of similar cells with specialized functions.

Muscle Tissue and Nerve Tissue

Your muscle tissue is the only kind of tissue that can contract, becoming shorter and thicker. This specialized ability makes possible all your movements. Three kinds of muscle tissue are discussed on pages 42–43.

Nerve tissue transmits electrical signals. Because your nerves have this specialized ability, they can carry messages to your brain from inside and outside your body. Your nerves also carry instructions from your brain back to all parts of your body. Nerve tissue is discussed on pages 70–71.

Epithelial Tissue

Epithelial cells join to form continuous sheets of tissue. They provide a covering for your whole body: the outer layer of your skin. They also line your hollow internal organs.

During the ordinary activities of life, your skin and these linings undergo much wear and tear. Fortunately, epithelial tissue has a special capacity to renew itself as old cells wear out.

Epithelial cells, all tightly packed together, come in various shapes. On the surface of your skin and in the lining of your blood vessels, they are shaped like overlapping shields. In the lining of your digestive and respiratory tracts, they are shaped like columns. The epithelial cells of glands are cube shaped. The bladder is lined with transitional cells, which change shape when they are stretched.

All epithelial tissues exposed to the air, except the cornea of the eye, are dry. They are protected by a tough protein called keratin. Inside your body, most epithelial surfaces are protected by a liquid film of mucus. For example, your mouth is lined with epithelial tissue. This kind of tissue continues down into your digestive and respiratory passages.

Glands, which are made up of epithelial cells, produce liquids or chemicals for use outside themselves. You have glands to produce mucus, saliva, sweat, hormones, and many other substances needed by your body.

Some epithelial tissue is only one cell thick. The walls of capillaries, the tubes of your kidneys, and many other parts of your body consist of this kind of epithelial

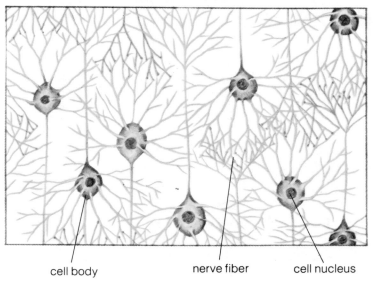

cell body   nerve fiber   cell nucleus

Nerve tissue, which transmits electrical signals, relays messages between your brain and all parts of your body.

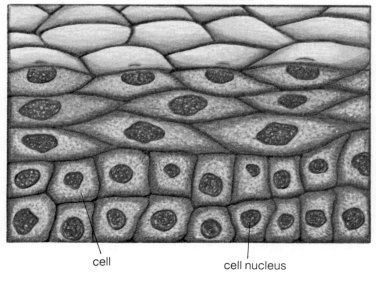

cell   cell nucleus

Epithelial tissue makes up the waterproof outer layer of your skin. It also lines your hollow internal organs.

tissue. It is so thin that water, oxygen, minerals, nutrients, and even blood cells can easily pass through.

Connective Tissue

Connective tissue connects, supports, and protects other tissues. Connective tissue contains relatively few cells, which are surrounded by a larger amount of nonliving material called the matrix.

Loose connective tissue is the commonest type. Its cells include fibroblasts, which produce different kinds of protein fibers, including collagen. Loose connective tissue is mostly found under the epidermis and around internal organs. It is the main packing material of your body. Fat tissue is often mixed with it.

Another kind of connective tissue forms tough cords, the ligaments and tendons, for your skeletal and muscular systems. This tissue is dense and sometimes elastic, consisting of tightly packed bundles of fibers.

Cartilage, a form of connective tissue, is white, flexible, and semitransparent. You can feel it in your outer ear or at the end of your nose. Cartilage forms the discs between the vertebrae of your spine, and it protects the ends of the bones that meet in your joints.

Cartilage forms a temporary skeleton for an unborn baby. It is gradually changed into bone as calcium and other minerals are laid down by living bone cells in the matrix of the cartilage.

muscle tissue
(with nerve fibers)   epithelial tissue

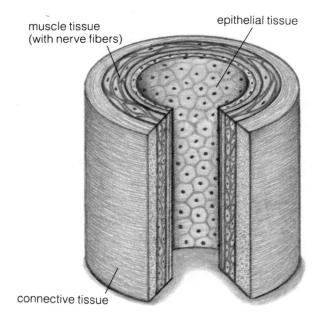

connective tissue

TISSUES COMBINE TO FORM ORGANS

The walls of an artery consist of different tissues working together to keep your blood flowing: elastic muscle tissue, nerve tissue, tough connective tissue for protection, and soft epithelial tissue for a smooth lining. Many of your organs consist of a variety of tissues, working together in different arrangements depending on the specialized function of each of the organs.

Cells

Your body contains trillions of cells. The average human cell is about 1/1,000 inch (.03 millimeter) wide. The shape and size of cells depend on the specialized work they perform.

In spite of this great variety, all cells have the same basic structure. A membrane encloses and protects the contents of the cell. It is flexible so that it can change shape easily. It is believed to consist of a mixture of loose proteins and layers of fatty substances. The membrane allows only certain substances to move in or out. Oxygen, nutrients, hormones, and proteins are taken into the cell only as needed. Wastes pass out through the membrane. Most cells have a nucleus, surrounded by a jellylike substance called cytoplasm.

The Nucleus

The nucleus is separated from the cytoplasm by a nuclear membrane similar to the outer membrane of the cell. The nucleus is the control center for the cell. It governs the specialized work performed by the cell and the cell's own growth, repair, and reproduction. The nucleus contains a network of threads called chromatin and a round mass, the nucleolus.

Some cells have two or more nuclei. If the nucleus or nuclei are destroyed, a cell will usually die in a short time. The red blood cell, which loses its nucleus at maturity, lives to carry oxygen for three to four months.

The Cytoplasm

Outside the nucleus, the cytoplasm fills the cell. The cytoplasm consists mostly of water with proteins dissolved in it. In the cytoplasm are many different structures called organelles (little organs).

Among the organelles are the mitochondria. These produce energy for the cell's own needs as well as its specialized work. The work of the mitochondria is aided by enzymes — proteins that speed up chemical changes.

Other important organelles are the ribosomes. They act as small factories. Here amino acids, already broken down from the proteins you eat, are assembled into the new proteins that your body needs.

Ribosomes may lie freely in the cytoplasm or may be attached to the endoplasmic reticulum. This is a network of channels, serving as a transport system between the cell membrane and the nuclear membrane.

Other organelles include lysosomes, sacs filled with digestive enzymes. These sacs help to digest food particles that have entered the cell through its outer membrane. Such particles become enclosed by small cavities called vacuoles. Lysosomes fuse with the vacuoles and digest the food. The cell absorbs what it can use. Undigested waste is released through the cell membrane.

Another system of organelles is a cluster of flat sacs called the Golgi apparatus. Here some proteins are stored, and some are packaged for use outside the cell.

SPECIALIZED WORK FOR YOUR CELLS
All the cells of your body perform specialized work. Some fight disease, transport oxygen, or produce movement. Others manufacture proteins, chemicals, or liquids. Some cells store nutrients. Others are responsible for your thoughts, emotions, and memories. The egg and sperm cells can combine to create new life.

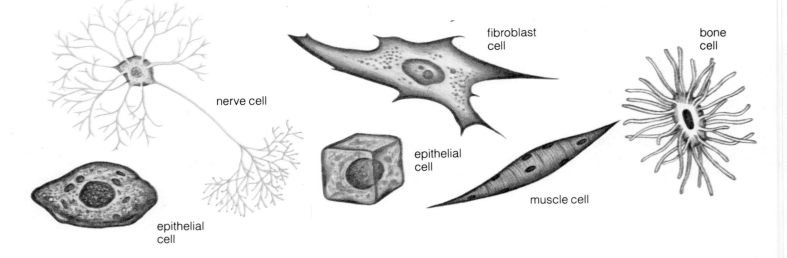

nerve cell

fibroblast cell

bone cell

epithelial cell

epithelial cell

muscle cell

THE CELL: BASIC UNIT OF LIFE

The cell duplicates in a simple way almost all the functions of the human body as a whole. The cell takes in food through its own skin, the membrane. It digests the food by using enzymes. It produces energy for work and heat. Most cells excrete wastes and can heal their own small wounds. Some can move to new locations. When there is need in the body, most cells can reproduce themselves exactly from the blueprint kept in their nucleus.

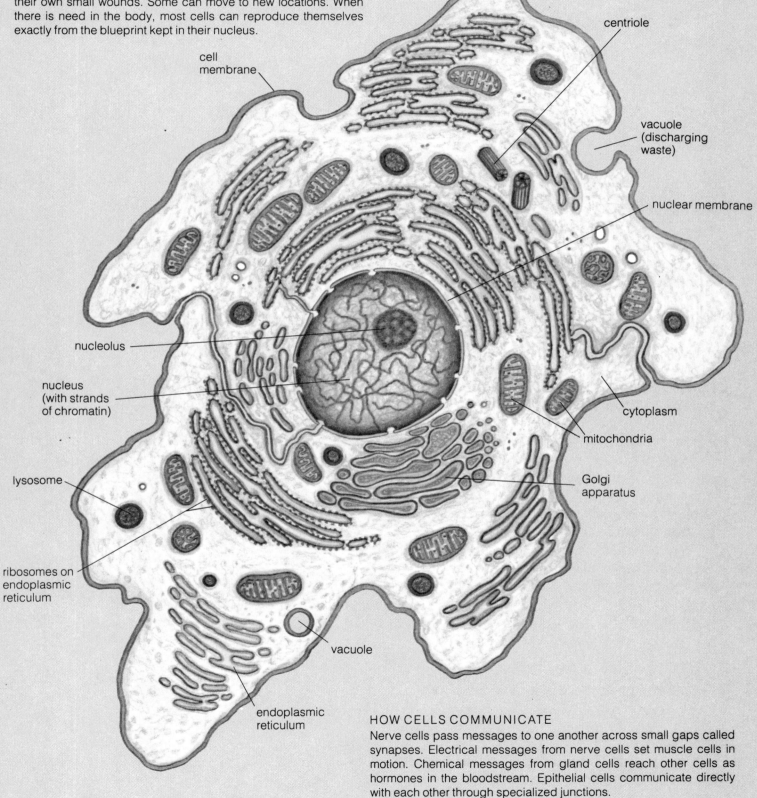

cell membrane

centriole

vacuole (discharging waste)

nuclear membrane

nucleolus

nucleus (with strands of chromatin)

cytoplasm

mitochondria

lysosome

Golgi apparatus

ribosomes on endoplasmic reticulum

vacuole

endoplasmic reticulum

HOW CELLS COMMUNICATE

Nerve cells pass messages to one another across small gaps called synapses. Electrical messages from nerve cells set muscle cells in motion. Chemical messages from gland cells reach other cells as hormones in the bloodstream. Epithelial cells communicate directly with each other through specialized junctions.

Skeletal System

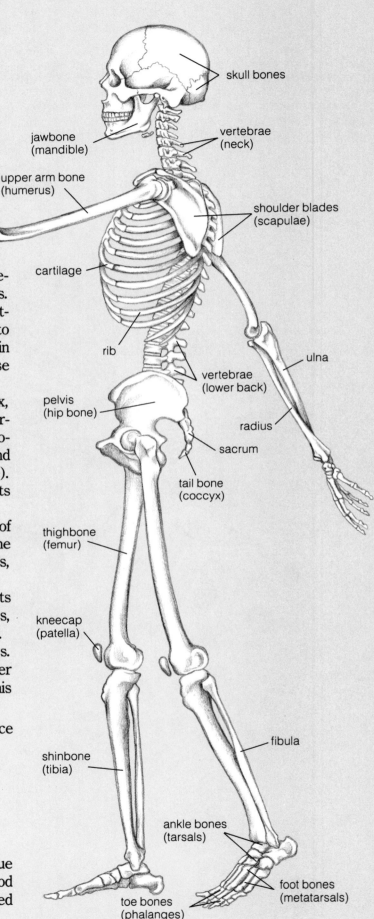

skull bones

jawbone (mandible)

vertebrae (neck)

upper arm bone (humerus)

shoulder blades (scapulae)

cartilage

rib

ulna

vertebrae (lower back)

pelvis (hip bone)

radius

sacrum

tail bone (coccyx)

thighbone (femur)

kneecap (patella)

fibula

shinbone (tibia)

ankle bones (tarsals)

foot bones (metatarsals)

toe bones (phalanges)

YOUR SKELETAL SYSTEM provides the framework for your body and protects delicate organs. Your bones enable you to stand upright. Muscles attached to the firm surfaces of your bones enable you to move. You cannot see your bones. But under your skin you can probably feel most of the bones shown in these drawings.

The 29 bones of your skull form a very strong box, protecting your brain, your eyes, and the most important parts of your ears. Your heart and lungs are protected by the rigid cage formed by your breastbone and the 24 ribs attached to the spinal column (backbone). The spinal column, consisting of 26 vertebrae, protects the nerves of your spinal cord.

The marrow of certain bones makes the red cells of your blood and some of the white blood cells. The bones themselves serve as storage places for minerals, especially calcium and phosphorus.

Your largest bone is the thighbone, which accounts for about a fourth of your height. Your smallest bones, less than a tenth of an inch long, are in the middle ear.

The adult skeleton consists of about 206 bones. (Some small bones in the hands and feet vary in number from person to person.) These can be divided in this way:

SKULL: 29 bones (including the bones of the face and the 3 tiny bones in each ear)

SPINE: 26 bones called vertebrae

RIBS AND BREASTBONE (sternum): 25 bones

SHOULDERS, ARMS, AND HANDS: 64 bones

PELVIS, LEGS, AND FEET: 62 bones

Bone contains living tissue. Because living tissue needs a constant supply of nutrients and oxygen, blood vessels supply your bones. Your bones are also supplied with nerves.

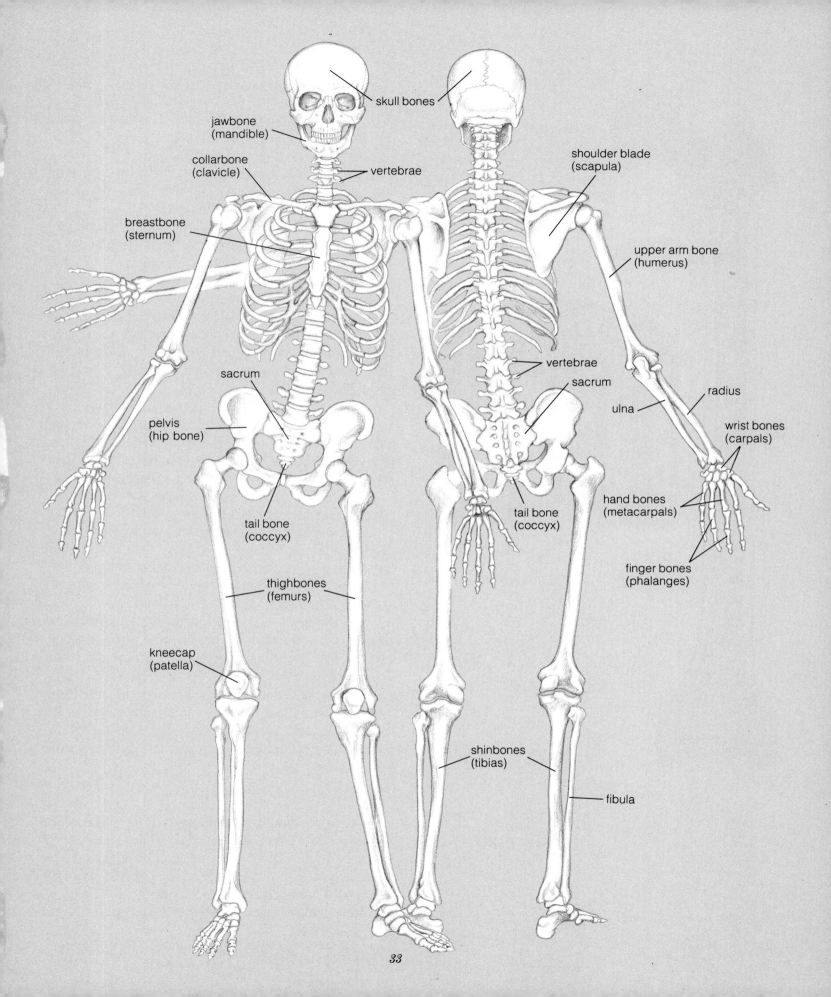

skull bones

jawbone
(mandible)

collarbone
(clavicle)

vertebrae

shoulder blade
(scapula)

breastbone
(sternum)

upper arm bone
(humerus)

sacrum

vertebrae

sacrum

radius

pelvis
(hip bone)

ulna

wrist bones
(carpals)

tail bone
(coccyx)

tail bone
(coccyx)

hand bones
(metacarpals)

thighbones
(femurs)

finger bones
(phalanges)

kneecap
(patella)

shinbones
(tibias)

fibula

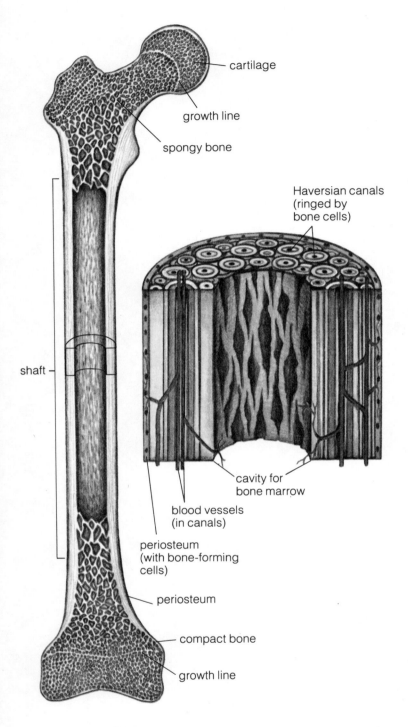

cartilage

growth line

spongy bone

Haversian canals
(ringed by
bone cells)

shaft

cavity for
bone marrow

blood vessels
(in canals)

periosteum
(with bone-forming
cells)

periosteum

compact bone

growth line

THE LIVING BONE

Much of bone consists of calcium, phosphorus, and other lifeless minerals. But about one-third of bone is living tissue. Like other cells, bone cells have their own blood supply to provide nutrients and oxygen and to remove wastes. The tough covering layer of a bone contains branching blood vessels that run through to canals within the bone.

Your Bones

Your bones are well designed for the work they do. They are strong but relatively light. They are hard, and yet flexible enough so that they are not easy to break. If a bone breaks, it repairs itself.

Each bone has a special size and shape, depending on the work it does and its location in your body. But all bones are made of the same materials.

Covering the bone is a tough membrane, the periosteum. It contains bone-forming cells and blood vessels bringing blood to the outer layer of bone.

This outer layer is called compact bone. It consists of many circular structures of mineral materials, surrounding tiny canals (Haversian canals). Bone cells lie between the circular structures. Through the canals, blood vessels bring food and oxygen to your bone cells. If you break a bone, nerves in the canals will inform your brain about the pain.

The inner layer of bone looks something like a honeycomb: it is a network of bone with spaces between. Although it is called spongy bone, it is just as strong as compact bone. If all your bones were compact, your skeleton would be enormously heavy.

In the center of many bones is space for red marrow, which manufactures most of your blood cells. About half a pound (227 grams) of red marrow produces about 5 billion red blood cells every day. Before birth, red marrow fills all the bones. But in an adult it is found only in the skull, breastbone, vertebrae, hip bones, and ends of the long bones.

The shafts of long bones contain yellow marrow, which is mostly made of fat. In case of emergency, yellow marrow may become red marrow and make blood cells.

Calcium, phosphorus, and other minerals are stored in the bones. These minerals can be removed from the bones and sent to other tissues through the bloodstream as needed. This exchange is regulated by the parathyroid glands.

Bone Growth

Your bones began to form, as cartilage, long before you were born. As you grow, this cartilage is gradually hardened into bone by the addition of minerals. The cartilage itself grows to enlarge the "model" on which the bone of an adult is finally formed.

Bone growth begins at the primary center of each

FROM CARTILAGE TO BONE

In the "temporary" skeleton of a three-year old (*above*), there is still much cartilage, which does not show up in an X ray. In the hand of an adult (*right*), all the skeletal cartilage has hardened into bone.

bones become softened and misshapen. Failure of the thyroid or pituitary glands to produce normal hormone levels will result in a very small body (dwarfism). An excess of growth hormone will result in a very large body (giantism).

Broken Bones

When a bone is broken, a blood clot forms between the pieces. Within a few days this clot is invaded by immature bone cells. They produce a callus — a lump of immature bone that surrounds the broken area and binds it together. Gradually the callus changes shape until the bone returns to its normal shape and strength. If the broken pieces of bone are not kept in the proper position during the healing process, the healed bone will be misshapen.

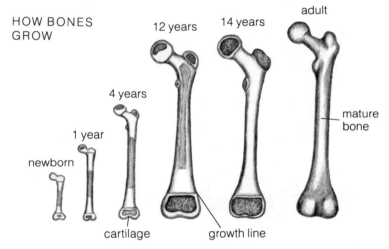

HOW BONES GROW

Cartilage forms the "model" for future bones. As the model continues to grow, it is gradually changed into hard bone.

bone. In a long bone, the primary center is in the middle of the shaft. Growth extends up and down around the central marrow cavity. Then secondary growth centers appear at both ends. Until full growth has been achieved, areas of cartilage remain between the areas of bone growth. These are called growth plates.

From an X ray of a child's hand, a doctor can see how much bone and how much growth plate are present. The doctor can then predict how much bone growth can be expected. In this way a child's adult height can be estimated in advance.

All growth stops when the growth plates are fully hardened into bone. In a young man, completion of growth is determined at about 18 to 21 years of age by a hormone from the testicles. In a young woman, completion of growth is determined at about 16 to 18 years of age by a hormone from the ovaries. Later a growth line remains, showing where the growth took place.

For healthy bone growth, the body as a whole must function well. Disease, poor nutrition, injury, or long inactivity may interfere with bone growth. Lack of enough vitamin D causes rickets, a disease in which

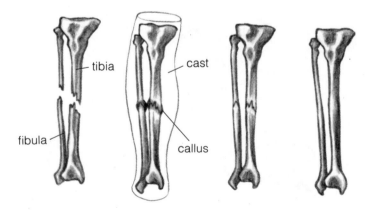

HOW BROKEN BONES HEAL

After a bone is broken, bone cells move into the space between the pieces. The cells produce immature bone (callus), which is later replaced by mature bone.

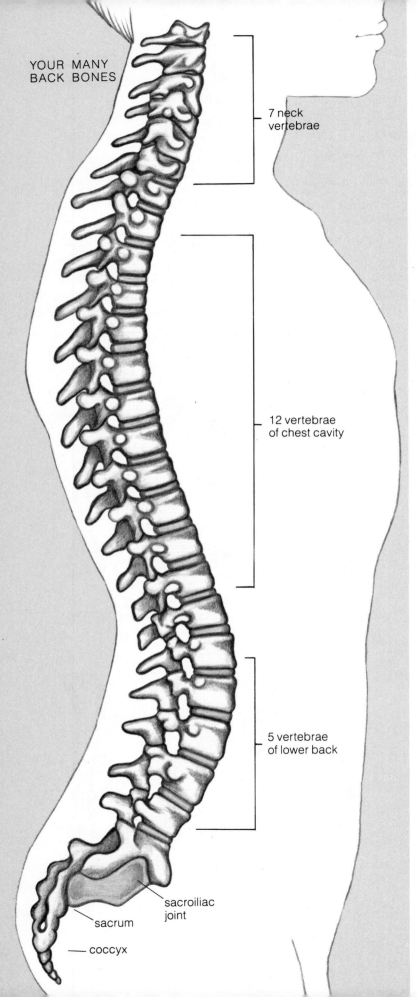

YOUR MANY
BACK BONES

7 neck
vertebrae

12 vertebrae
of chest cavity

5 vertebrae
of lower back

sacroiliac
joint

sacrum

coccyx

Your Spine

The central support for your entire body is your spine, also known as the backbone. It actually consists of many small bones called vertebrae. They are held together by ligaments. Your ribs curve out from the vertebrae of your chest cavity. Because your lower vertebrae bear more weight, they are thicker and heavier than the vertebrae higher up.

Running through the back part of your vertebrae is your spinal cord, an important organ of your nervous system. The cord is about 18 inches (45 centimeters) long in an adult, reaching from the brain to just below the lowest vertebra of the chest cavity.

Between each two vertebrae is a disc of softer cartilage. These spinal discs are shock absorbers for the delicate brain at the top of your spine. When you sit or stand, your discs are squeezed together. So you are one-fourth to one-half inch shorter before you go to bed than when you get up.

Because your spinal discs are somewhat flexible, they allow you to bend and turn your backbone in many directions. You can reach for a book on a high shelf, bend down to tie your shoelaces, or swing a tennis racket.

Sometimes a disc will squeeze out beyond the vertebrae, pressing painfully on a nearby nerve. This is called a slipped disc. Bed rest may ease the pain. Strengthening the back muscles may compensate for the weakness of the disc.

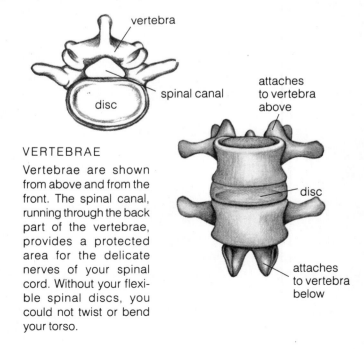

vertebra

spinal canal

disc

attaches
to vertebra
above

disc

attaches
to vertebra
below

VERTEBRAE

Vertebrae are shown from above and from the front. The spinal canal, running through the back part of the vertebrae, provides a protected area for the delicate nerves of your spinal cord. Without your flexible spinal discs, you could not twist or bend your torso.

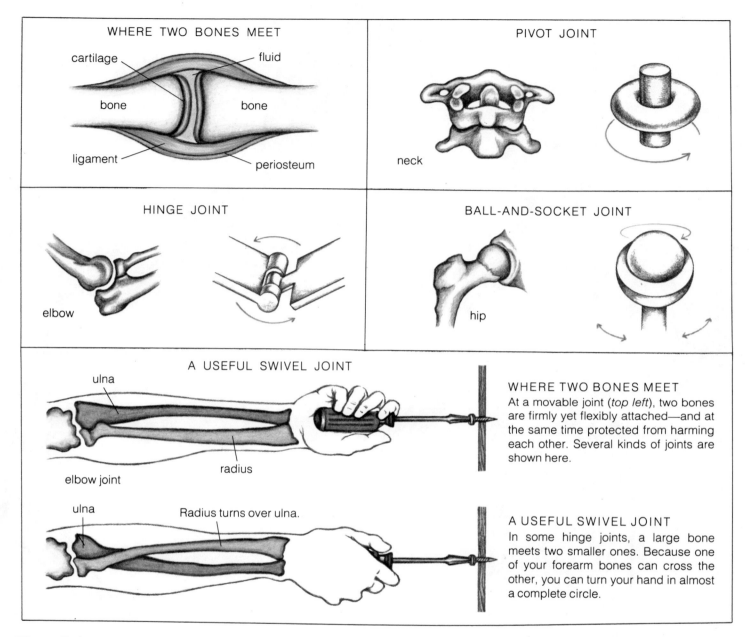

WHERE TWO BONES MEET

cartilage
fluid
bone
bone
ligament
periosteum

PIVOT JOINT

neck

HINGE JOINT

elbow

BALL-AND-SOCKET JOINT

hip

A USEFUL SWIVEL JOINT

ulna
radius
elbow joint

ulna
Radius turns over ulna.

WHERE TWO BONES MEET
At a movable joint (*top left*), two bones are firmly yet flexibly attached—and at the same time protected from harming each other. Several kinds of joints are shown here.

A USEFUL SWIVEL JOINT
In some hinge joints, a large bone meets two smaller ones. Because one of your forearm bones can cross the other, you can turn your hand in almost a complete circle.

Your Joints

A joint occurs where two bones meet. A bone can't bend, but most joints can. To bend or turn or twist any part of your body, you need a joint.

Your hip joints, shoulder joints, and thumb joints allow movement in many directions. Other joints allow only limited movements. The joints in your skull have grown together so tightly that they allow no movement at all.

In a movable joint, ligaments and muscles hold the two bones together. The ends of the bones are coated with very smooth cartilage so that they won't injure each other. Surrounding the joint is a capsule containing a special fluid. Like oil in a mechanical joint, the fluid prevents friction between the two bones. Some joints also have small sacs, called bursae, filled with fluid. The bursae act as shock absorbers. If they are injured, the result is bursitis.

If you force a joint beyond the limits of the ligaments, they will tear, and you will have a sprain. If the joint is pulled out of its normal position, it is said to be dislocated. The dislocation may result from weakness or a tear in a joint capsule. When the ligaments are very flexible, a joint may have an unusually wide range of movement. This is sometimes called being double jointed.

Arthritis results from damage to a joint. It may come from infection, injury, disease, or wear and tear over the years.

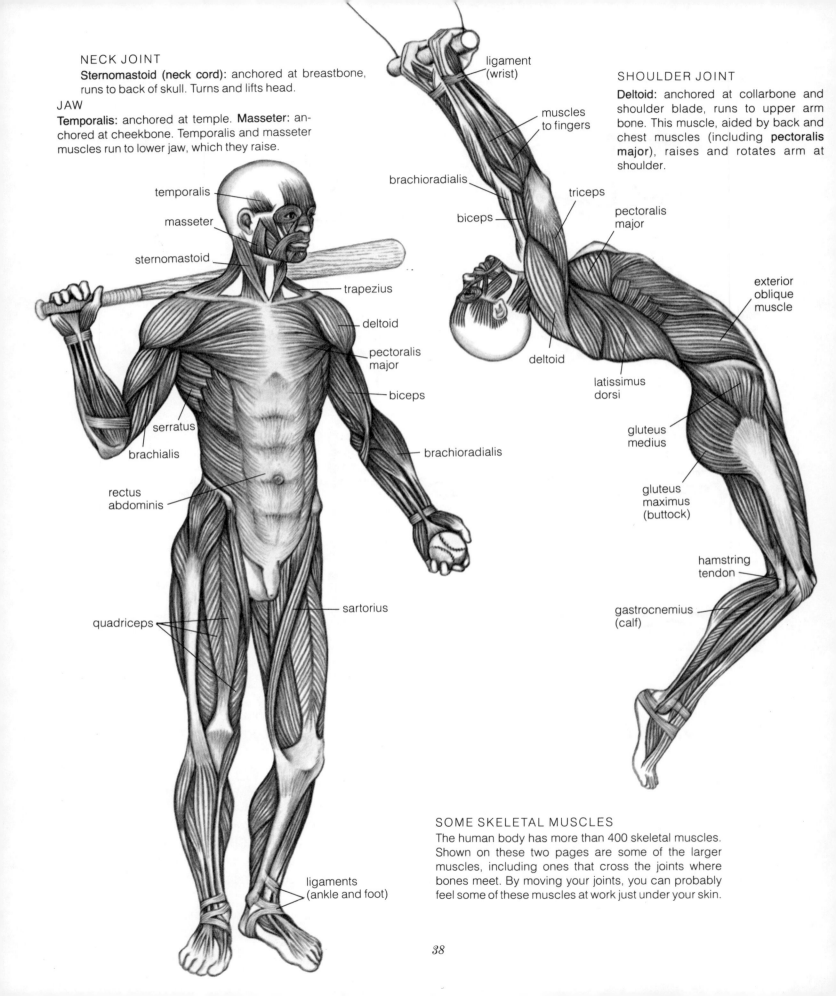

NECK JOINT
Sternomastoid (neck cord): anchored at breastbone, runs to back of skull. Turns and lifts head.

JAW
Temporalis: anchored at temple. **Masseter:** anchored at cheekbone. Temporalis and masseter muscles run to lower jaw, which they raise.

ligament (wrist)

muscles to fingers

brachioradialis

biceps

temporalis

masseter

sternomastoid

trapezius

deltoid

pectoralis major

biceps

serratus

brachialis

rectus abdominis

quadriceps

sartorius

brachioradialis

ligaments (ankle and foot)

SHOULDER JOINT
Deltoid: anchored at collarbone and shoulder blade, runs to upper arm bone. This muscle, aided by back and chest muscles (including **pectoralis major**), raises and rotates arm at shoulder.

triceps

pectoralis major

exterior oblique muscle

deltoid

latissimus dorsi

gluteus medius

gluteus maximus (buttock)

hamstring tendon

gastrocnemius (calf)

SOME SKELETAL MUSCLES
The human body has more than 400 skeletal muscles. Shown on these two pages are some of the larger muscles, including ones that cross the joints where bones meet. By moving your joints, you can probably feel some of these muscles at work just under your skin.

Muscular System

WE HAVE THREE KINDS of muscles. Skeletal muscles are attached to our bones, enabling us to bend and twist our joints. These muscles control every move we make — from disco dancing to driving a car, from moving furniture to writing a letter, from playing a video game to blinking our eyes.

In a man's body, the skeletal muscles make up more than 40 percent of his weight. In the body of a woman, the proportion of muscle tissue is lower and the proportion of fat tissue is greater than in a man. The smallest skeletal muscles are the tiny muscles of the middle ear, which are barely visible. The largest skeletal muscle is the huge gluteus maximus, which forms the largest part of the buttock.

In addition to our skeletal muscles, other muscles control movements of the internal systems of the body — our digestive, circulatory, urinary, and reproductive systems. Through movements we hardly notice, muscles keep these systems working efficiently, even when we are asleep. Most of this activity is the work of our smooth muscles. The third kind of muscle, found only in the heart, is called cardiac muscle.

Muscles consist mostly of protein. Some people refer to muscles as "flesh" or "meat on the bones." When we eat meat or fish, we are eating animal muscle.

ELBOW JOINT

Biceps: anchored at shoulder blade. **Brachialis:** anchored at upper arm bone. Both muscles run to forearm bones. These muscles raise, bend, and twist arm at elbow. **Triceps:** anchored at shoulder blade and upper arm bone. **Brachioradialis:** anchored at upper arm bone. Both muscles run to forearm bones. These muscles lower, straighten, and twist arm at elbow.

HIP JOINT

Gluteus maximus (buttock): anchored at pelvis, runs to thighbone. Rotates and extends thigh.

ANKLE JOINT

Gastrocnemius (calf): anchored at lower part of thighbone, runs to heel bone via Achilles tendon. Helps to bend knee and lift heel off ground.

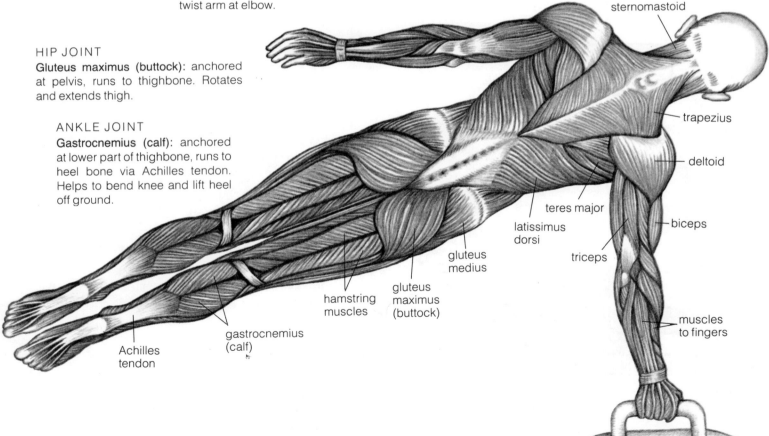

sternomastoid

trapezius

deltoid

teres major

latissimus dorsi

biceps

triceps

gluteus medius

muscles to fingers

gluteus maximus (buttock)

hamstring muscles

gastrocnemius (calf)

Achilles tendon

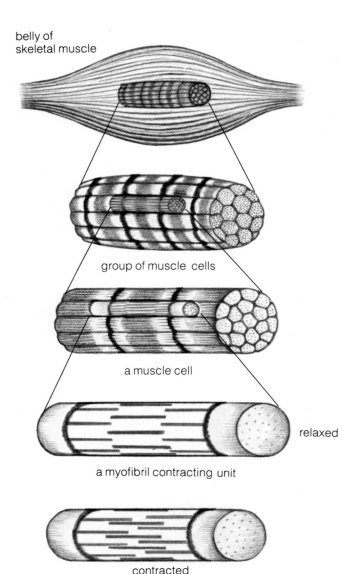

belly of
skeletal muscle

group of muscle cells

a muscle cell

a myofibril contracting unit

relaxed

contracted

HOW A MUSCLE CELL CONTRACTS

The belly, or body, of a skeletal muscle contains many muscle cells, or muscle fibers (of which only 15 are shown here). Each cell contains many myofibrils (of which only 20 are shown here). The myofibrils contain two main kinds of protein. When these proteins overlap, the muscle cell becomes shorter and thicker.

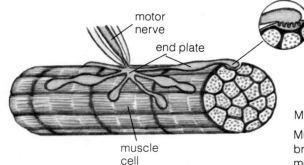

motor
nerve

end plate

muscle
cell

Your Skeletal Muscles

Your skeletal muscles enable you to move your body. They come in many different shapes, specialized for their different functions. Most of them are rather long and thin. Many skeletal muscles are attached to bones on both sides of a joint so that the bones can be moved. These muscles are often arranged in pairs. One muscle bends the joint, and the other straightens it. Such pairs of muscles are called antagonists because they oppose each other's motion. To achieve full movement, one muscle must relax as the opposite one contracts. If both antagonists contract at the same time, no movement occurs.

Some muscles are flat. Your diaphragm, the main muscle for breathing, is a flat muscle. Some of the muscles of your face are attached not to bone but to skin. The sphincter muscles that enable you to close your anus and other openings are completely circular.

The muscles in your back help to stabilize your spinal column so that you can stand upright. Leg muscles help you to stand, shift your weight, run, and jump.

Since your arms do not have to support the weight of your body, their muscles are smaller than those of your legs. But the muscles of your arms and legs are arranged in similar ways.

Muscles also serve to protect your delicate internal organs. Your abdomen cannot be surrounded by bones, as your chest cavity is. The reason is that your stomach swells after a meal, and a woman's uterus swells when she is pregnant. So your abdomen is protected by three layers of strong muscle.

Muscles often attach themselves to bones through tendons. The muscles of your fingers actually start at the upper part of the lower arm. It is their very long tendons, leading to each individual finger, that you see and feel through the skin on the back of your hand.

The contraction of a muscle is triggered by a chemical process. This makes the myofibrils of a muscle cell slide over each other to shorten the cell. The chemical process involves two proteins, myosin and actin, that give skeletal muscles a striped (striated) appearance under the microscope.

MESSAGE FROM YOUR NERVOUS SYSTEM

Muscle cells contract because of nerve impulses. Each cell is served by a branch of a motor nerve. On the surface of the cell, the nerve branch forms a motor end plate. When the nerve is stimulated, it releases a chemical (neurotransmitter) in the tiny space between the end plate and the muscle cell. This chemical stimulates the cell to contract. When the neurotransmitter is used up, the contraction stops.

A muscle can be shortened by up to one third of its resting length. Each muscle cell that contracts does so completely. For a stronger contraction, more cells are stimulated to contract. As a muscle gets shorter, it also gets thicker. If you bend your elbow, you can feel the swelling of the biceps in your upper arm.

The work of your muscles requires energy. This is supplied by glucose, which usually comes from the carbohydrates you eat. The glucose may be stored in the muscles themselves, or your bloodstream may bring glucose to your muscles from other parts of your body. In order to release energy, the glucose must combine with oxygen, which is brought by red cells in your bloodstream.

During exercise the amount of oxygen supplied to the muscles might not be enough. Then a chemical, lactic acid, builds up, perhaps causing a muscle cramp. To eliminate the lactic acid, the muscle must continue to use oxygen even after its movement has stopped. After strenuous exercise, you pant — to provide the extra oxygen you still need.

There are two types of skeletal muscle cells, red cells and white cells. The red muscle cells can work longer than the white cells, but the white cells exert more force over a short time. In the human body these cells are mixed together, but in other animals, such as birds, whole muscles may be made of one type of cell. That is why there are white meat (white cells) and dark meat (red cells) in a chicken.

Exercise cannot increase the number of your muscle cells, but it increases the size of the individual cells. If muscles are not used, their size decreases.

How You Scratch Your Nose

Your skeletal muscles work under the control of your central nervous system. What happens if you want to scratch your nose?

Your brain cells send a message through your spinal cord and motor nerves to muscle cells. The muscles that bend your arm are told to contract.

Information returns to your brain from the muscles and joints, so that just the right amount of strength will be used to bring your hand up to your face — and no farther. Additional messages go back to the muscles that bend and stretch your finger.

There you are, scratching your nose. If your nervous system were less efficient, you might punch yourself in the face instead.

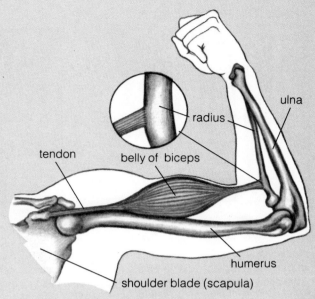

BONE TO MUSCLE TO BONE

A skeletal muscle is anchored to a firm bone. It runs across the joint to another bone, whose movement it controls. The muscle and its tendons have a sheath of connective tissue, which merges with the periosteum of each bone.

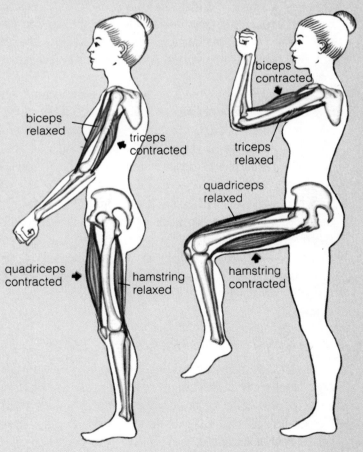

MUSCLES WORKING IN PAIRS

In your upper arm, a pair of antagonist muscles bend or straighten your elbow. In your upper leg, a similar pair of antagonists bend or straighten your knee. Other antagonists lift or lower your arm at the shoulder, and your leg at the hip.

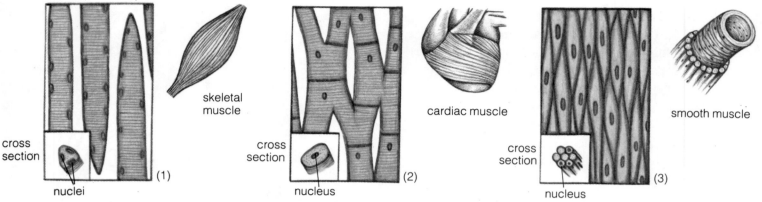

skeletal muscle

cardiac muscle

smooth muscle

cross section

nuclei

(1)

cross section

nucleus

(2)

cross section

nucleus

(3)

(1) Skeletal muscles, which move your joints, consist of long, striped muscle cells (fibers). Each muscle cell contains several nuclei. (2) Cardiac muscle forms the powerful wall of the heart. The muscle tissue consists of a network of striped muscle cells that are shorter than skeletal muscle cells. Each cell contains one nucleus. (3) Smooth muscles are important in the work of your internal systems. They consist of short muscle cells that are not striped. Each cell contains one nucleus.

Different Muscles for Different Work

The three types of muscles in your body look different under the microscope. The skeletal muscles are striped (striated). Each skeletal muscle cell contains many nuclei. Skeletal muscle cells are able to contract more fully than cardiac or smooth muscle cells. So skeletal muscles are suited to the large movements of your bones.

Cardiac muscles have a less striped appearance, and the cells contain only one nucleus each. The cardiac muscles have to be the strongest since they never stop working. In an average adult, they contract and relax between 60 and 100 times a minute. Cardiac muscle works day and night to pump blood through the body.

Smooth muscle cells have no striping. They are generally smaller than skeletal or cardiac muscle cells. Each smooth muscle cell usually contains only one nucleus. They contract rather slowly and smoothly, and they can remain contracted for long periods. Smooth muscles aid the work of several of your body's internal systems.

Voluntary and Involuntary Muscles

Skeletal muscles are under your own voluntary control. Some, such as your breathing muscles, perform most of the time without your being aware of them. Nevertheless you can, at least briefly, control these muscles. For example, you control your breathing muscles when you swim or hold your breath.

To take a step or draw a picture you need to use many of your skeletal muscles. Although you do not consciously plan every movement, your brain sends specific messages to each muscle. Your brain also receives messages back from the muscle whenever you make a movement. Complex movements such as driving a car or ice skating become easier and more efficient if they are repeated over and over.

Smooth muscles and cardiac muscles are not under your voluntary control. They are influenced by the part of your nervous system called the autonomic nervous system (page 68). If you get very nervous, your pupils may contract, your heart muscles may work faster, and your bladder muscles may contract, giving you the urge to urinate. Your control over these reactions is quite limited.

Muscles for Your Body's Systems

In your digestive tract, you have muscles in the walls of your esophagus, stomach, and intestines. Some of the muscle cells are circular, and others run lengthwise. By contracting, they squeeze the food and push it forward.

In your respiratory system, smooth muscles arranged in a circular pattern help to control the width of the air passages. If they contract too much, breathing becomes difficult. This is what happens during an asthma attack.

Your circulatory system is regulated by smooth muscles in the walls of your blood vessels. These can be narrowed by contraction or opened wide by relaxation.

In this way your blood pressure is regulated by your autonomic nervous system, and your blood can flow to the organs that need it most. The cardiac muscle cells form the heart, the pump that keeps the blood flowing through your circulatory system throughout your lifetime.

In your urinary system, smooth muscles in the ureters keep urine flowing from the kidneys to the bladder. The bladder itself has smooth muscles in its wall. When you urinate, these muscles contract to push the urine out. Where the bladder meets the urethra, a smooth, ringlike muscle keeps the opening closed except during urination. A similar ring of skeletal muscle further helps you to control urination.

In the female reproductive system, smooth muscles in the fallopian tubes ensure that the egg cell is transported to the uterus from the ovary. The uterus has very strong muscles. By contracting, they expel the uterine lining during the menstrual period, and they push out the baby during childbirth.

Keeping Your Muscles Healthy

In order to build up your muscles and keep them in shape, you must eat proteins. Not only meat and fish but many types of vegetables and grains contain proteins.

Your muscles are constantly at work. Even in your sleep you keep breathing, your heart keeps pumping, and the smooth muscles of your internal systems continue working. To perform all this work your muscles need a constant supply of nutrients in the form of glucose. The more you exercise, the more food you need to provide energy for your muscles.

Your muscles are strongest at about age 25, but through exercise they can be kept strong long after this. Without exercise they tend to become smaller and weaker. Exercise also helps to increase the glycogen content of your muscles. Glycogen is the form in which glucose is stored so as to be available for use when needed. With more glycogen available, your muscles can function more easily since they do not have to wait for glucose brought to them through the bloodstream.

The combination of exercise with a healthy diet will give greater strength and stamina to your muscles — and to you.

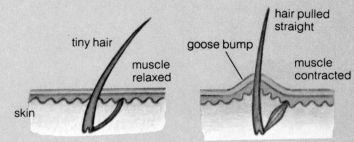

TINY MUSCLES FOR HAIRS

Each hair on the skin is supplied by a small bundle of involuntary muscle cells. When the muscle is contracted, it raises the hair and produces a "goose bump."

HOW YOU SMILE

Some muscles that make you smile are anchored at your cheekbones. By contracting, they lift the corners of your mouth.

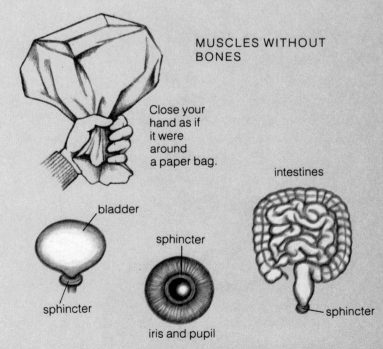

MUSCLES WITHOUT BONES

Close your hand as if it were around a paper bag.

Sphincter muscles form rings around some of your body's openings. By contracting, these muscles close the openings. In bright sunlight, a sphincter muscle makes your pupil smaller to keep the light from damaging your eye.

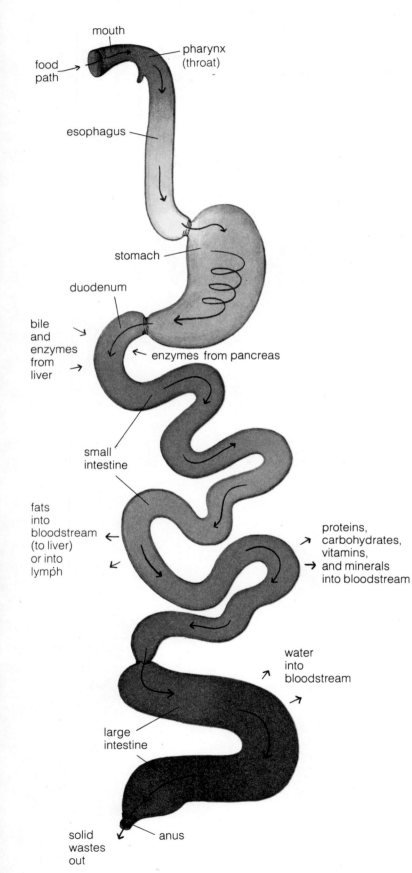

mouth

food path

pharynx (throat)

esophagus

stomach

duodenum

bile and enzymes from liver

enzymes from pancreas

small intestine

fats into bloodstream (to liver) or into lymph

proteins, carbohydrates, vitamins, and minerals into bloodstream

water into bloodstream

large intestine

anus

solid wastes out

Digestive System

E VERY CELL IN the body, from a four-foot-long nerve cell to the smallest sperm cell, performs work. Work requires energy, and energy consumes fuel. Fuel for your body's energy comes from the food you eat — carbohydrates, proteins, and fats. Your food also provides raw materials for building, repairing, and controlling your body systems.

The digestive system is truly a remarkable machine. During a person's lifetime, it may process between 60,000 and 100,000 pounds of food.

Processing Your Food

Digestion breaks down food into nutrients — basic materials the body can use. This process takes place chiefly in the alimentary canal, a long tube beginning at the mouth and ending at the anus. In adults the canal is about 27 feet long. The liver and pancreas aid in the work of digestion.

You might think of your digestive system as a giant food processor that breaks down your food both mechanically and chemically. Mechanically, the food is chopped, mashed, and mixed into a soupy paste. Chemically, digestive juices break down its contents into nutrients.

For example, proteins are made up of subunits called amino acids, which are linked together like the beads of a necklace. The enzymes of your alimentary canal break the links between the amino acids. The amino acids are absorbed into the bloodstream and carried to other parts of your body. There they are rearranged into new protein chains that enable your body to grow and to function.

WHAT HAPPENS TO THE FOOD YOU EAT

Your alimentary canal is a tube beginning at your mouth and ending at your anus. In the average adult it is about 27 feet long, with many twists and turns. Your stomach can enlarge to become much wider than the rest of the canal. Your esophagus is the narrowest part of the canal.

From the food you eat, your digestive system extracts the nutrients needed by the tissues and organs of your body. Material you cannot digest passes out through your rectum.

Circular muscles called sphincters open and close to control the passage of food through your body. A meal usually takes 15 hours to 2 days to pass through your alimentary canal.

Carbohydrates also consist of long chains of simpler subunits — starches and sugars. There are many different kinds of sugars (including sucrose, better known as table sugar). The body can only use one kind of sugar for energy: glucose. The carbohydrate chains in food must therefore be chopped up into their subunits, which are then converted into glucose.

Digestion from the Top

Even before you take a bite, the smell and sight of appetizing food begins the process of digestion. Your salivary glands start producing the digestive juices called saliva, so that your mouth waters. Your esophagus begins to ripple in anticipation of moving food from your throat to your stomach. Meanwhile your stomach produces digestive juices in preparation for digestion.

After you bite into a hamburger, the food is cooled (or warmed) to body temperature by the blood-rich lining of your mouth. Your teeth chop and grind the food into smaller pieces. Your tongue mashes the food against your hard palate, the roof of your mouth, in order to mix it with saliva. Then your tongue, which is your most flexible muscle, moves the food into position for more chewing.

Your saliva moistens and softens the food. The saliva contains a special enzyme, which begins the chemical breakdown of the carbohydrates in your food.

Now your tongue moves the food to the back of your mouth to be swallowed.

Ready-made Nutrients

Food also delivers vitamins and minerals. Your body absorbs and uses them in the same form in which they arrive in your food. Some vitamins are absorbed with fat, whereas others are dissolved in water and absorbed.

Minerals originally come from nonliving (inorganic) sources. They play vital roles in your body. For example, your bones and teeth are made largely of calcium and other minerals. You need iron for healthy blood. You need sodium and potassium for normal functioning of your nerves and muscles.

Vitamins originally come from living (organic) sources — plants and animals. They are just as important as minerals. For example, you need vitamin D for strong bones and teeth. You need vitamin A in order to see in dim light.

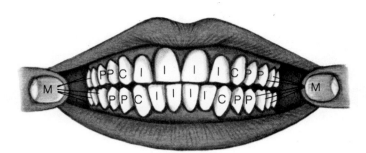

SPECIALIZED TEETH FOR SPECIAL JOBS

The incisors (I) are shaped like knives for cutting and slicing. The canines (C) have points for piercing and tearing. The premolars (P) and molars (M) have broad, bumpy surfaces for grinding. An adult has 32 teeth, but the four wisdom teeth are often removed to avoid crowding.

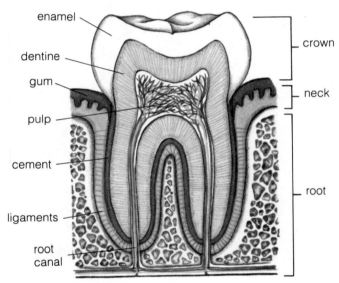

INSIDE A TOOTH

Ligaments and natural cement hold a tooth in place in your gum. The tooth is covered with the hardest material in your body: enamel. Under the enamel is a softer layer, dentine. The inner pulp contains blood and lymph vessels and nerves. Pain from a nerve often provides warning of decay, giving time to repair the damage and save the tooth.

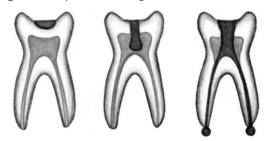

THREE STAGES OF TOOTH DECAY

(1) Bacteria eat through the hard enamel, creating a cavity. (2) If the cavity is not repaired, the bacteria invade through the dentine into the pulp. The infection stimulates a nerve, causing toothache. (3) The entire pulp and even the root canal may become infected. The tooth may die.

hard palate

teeth

soft palate

nasal cavity

tongue

salivary duct

salivary glands

pharynx (throat)

esophagus

sphincter

DIGESTING PROTEINS

Meat, fish, milk, eggs, whole grains, and beans supply your body with proteins—chains of amino acids. In your alimentary canal the protein molecules begin to break down into separate amino acids, which your bloodstream carries to other parts of your body. There the amino acids are rearranged into the new proteins that your cells need.

Many amino acids become the raw materials for building new cells and tissues (such as skin) or for repair of old ones. Proteins are especially important while the body is growing, but adults still need them to repair cells and tissues.

DIGESTING CARBOHYDRATES

Vegetables, fruits, bread, and cereals supply your body with starches and sugars, called carbohydrates. In your mouth the carbohydrates begin to break down into simple sugars such as glucose. (If you chew a salt cracker long enough, it will begin to taste sweet.) The digestion of carbohydrates is completed in your small intestine.

Your bloodstream carries the glucose to other parts of your body. Your cells can use the glucose right away for energy. Or the glucose may be stored in your liver and muscles until it is needed elsewhere in your body.

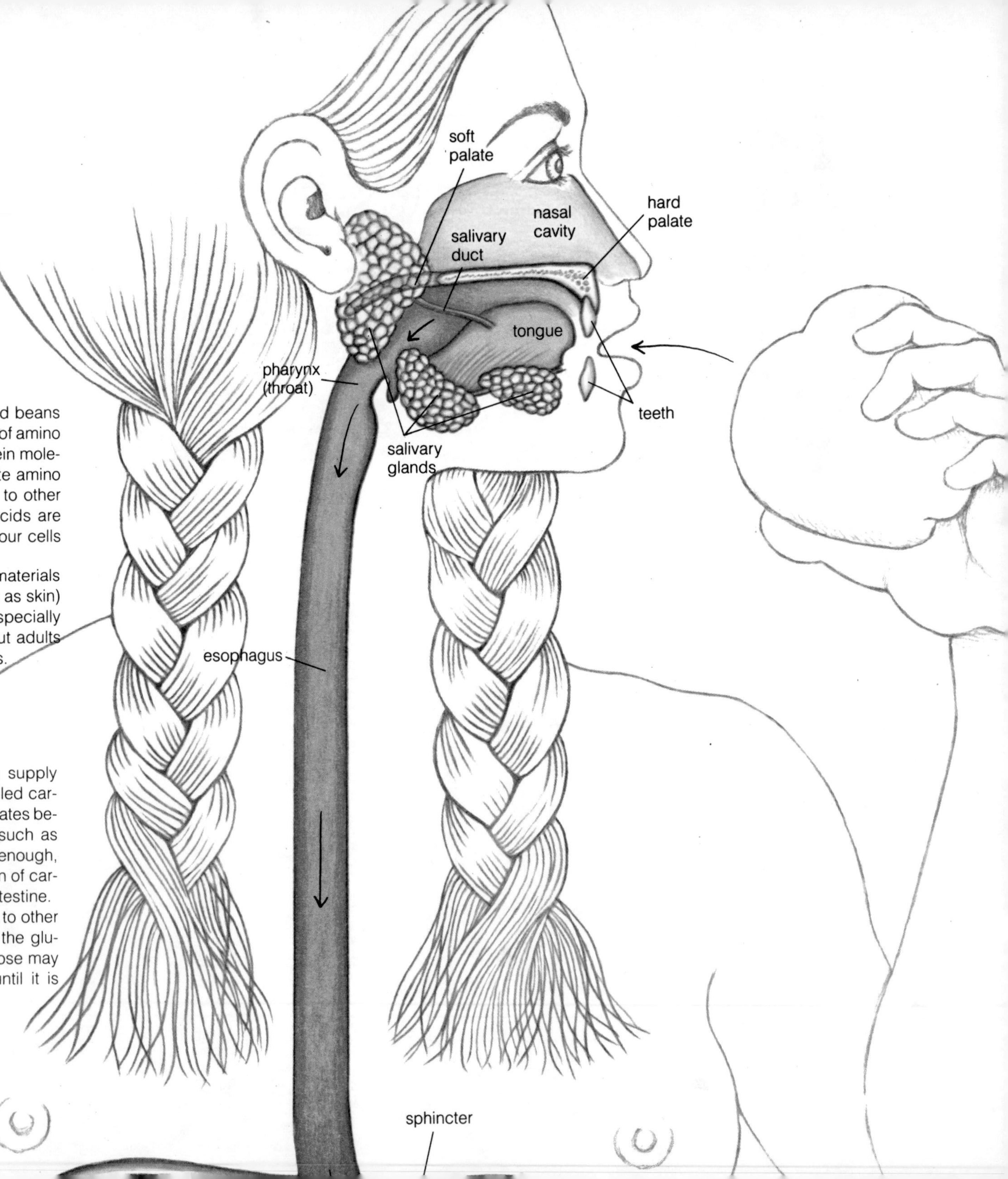

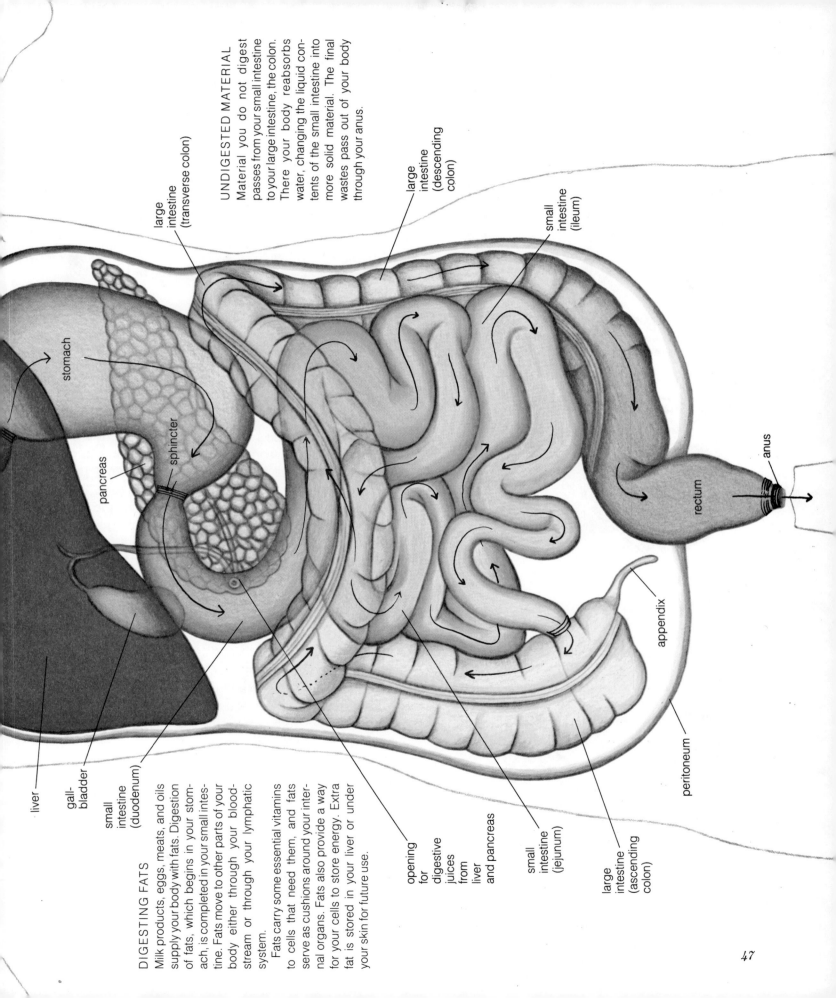

large intestine (transverse colon)

UNDIGESTED MATERIAL
Material you do not digest passes from your small intestine to your large intestine, the colon. There your body reabsorbs water, changing the liquid contents of the small intestine into more solid material. The final wastes pass out of your body through your anus.

large intestine (descending colon)

small intestine (ileum)

stomach

pancreas

sphincter

anus

liver

gall-bladder

small intestine (duodenum)

rectum

appendix

peritoneum

DIGESTING FATS
Milk products, eggs, meats, and oils supply your body with fats. Digestion of fats, which begins in your stomach, is completed in your small intestine. Fats move to other parts of your body either through your bloodstream or through your lymphatic system.

Fats carry some essential vitamins to cells that need them, and fats serve as cushions around your internal organs. Fats also provide a way for your cells to store energy. Extra fat is stored in your liver or under your skin for future use.

opening for digestive juices from liver and pancreas

small intestine (jejunum)

large intestine (ascending colon)

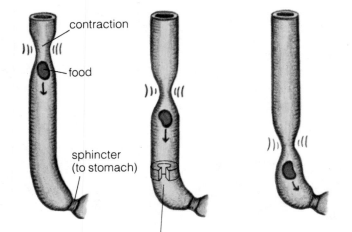

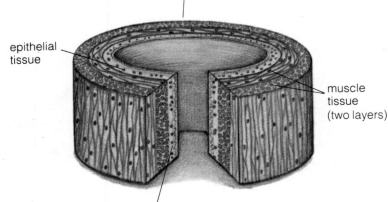

PERISTALSIS: WAVES OF CONTRACTION
With waves of contraction known as peristalsis, the muscular walls of your esophagus push your food along to your stomach.

TISSUES OF YOUR ALIMENTARY CANAL
The enlarged cross section shows that your esophagus wall contains two layers of muscle tissue. The inner layer is circular, and the outer layer runs lengthwise. The two layers, working together in peristalsis, move your food along. Like your esophagus, most of your alimentary canal has a wall of muscle tissue, a covering of connective tissue, and a lining of epithelial tissue.

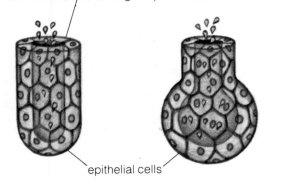

GLANDS
The lining of the esophagus contains glands producing mucus. A gland is an organ made of epithelial cells that produces a chemical or liquid for use outside itself. Other parts of the alimentary canal contain glands that are similar in structure to the mucous glands but produce digestive juices.

Swallowing Your Food

Swallowing forces a ball of food into your pharynx (throat). You stop breathing and talking for a moment. A trapdoor called the epiglottis automatically closes the opening to your voice box and lungs. The back part of the roof of your mouth, the soft palate, swings up to shut off the nasal passage. The food therefore has nowhere to go but down your esophagus.

If you swallow too fast, your epiglottis may not have time to close completely. Then you automatically cough to clear out any food particles that might have entered your trachea (windpipe).

Your Esophagus

The ball of food goes down your esophagus. This is a strong, muscular tube, about 10 inches long in an adult, connecting the pharynx (throat) with the stomach. When the esophagus is empty, it is flattened from front to back.

In your neck, the esophagus lies behind your trachea (windpipe) and in front of your spine. It passes through your chest cavity, behind your heart. Then it passes through your diaphragm.

Like the rest of your alimentary canal, the wall of your esophagus has layers of muscle that squeeze the food along. A circular layer of muscle tissue, by contracting, narrows your esophagus. A lengthwise layer of muscle tissue, by contracting, shortens a section of the esophagus wall. The result is a rippling, wavelike motion called peristalsis.

Peristalsis can carry food from your throat to your stomach in about 10 seconds. The action of peristalsis is controlled by your autonomic nervous system.

Peristalsis is so efficient that you can swallow food or fluids even when you are upside down. Peristalsis reverses when you vomit, enabling your body to get rid of the rejected food in a hurry.

Your Stomach

The stomach is a kind of elastic bag, which can expand after a big meal to hold 2½ pints (1.2 liters) of food. Your stomach fits under your diaphragm on the left side of your abdomen, protected by your five lowest ribs. Food usually remains here for two to four hours while your stomach continues the digestive process begun in your mouth.

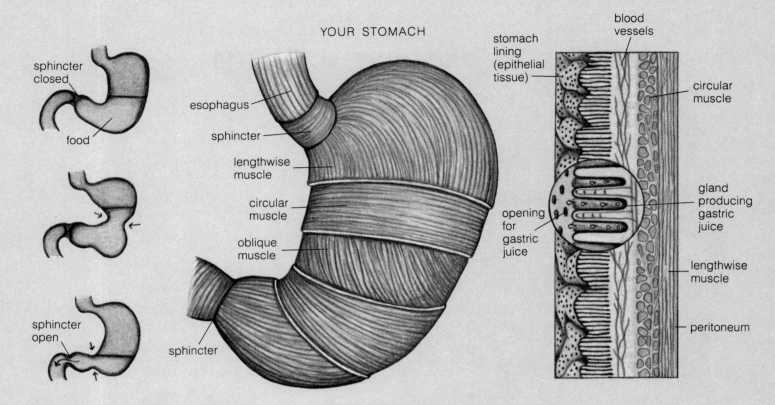

(1) A sphincter muscle controls the movement of partly digested food out of your stomach. When the duodenum is ready to receive a new batch of food, the sphincter opens. Through the action of peristalsis, your strong stomach muscles squeeze food out through the sphincter. (2) The muscle layers of the stomach wall are cut away here to show the three layers: lengthwise muscle, circular muscle, and oblique (slanting) muscle. Using these muscles the stomach can churn food up before moving it along into the duodenum. (3) This enlarged cross section of the stomach wall shows the layers of lengthwise and circular muscle. (The layer of oblique muscle is not shown here.) Blood vessels bring nutrients and oxygen to the stomach.

Your stomach contracts and expands, churning the food and mixing it well with digestive juices. Production of the digestive juices is stimulated by the smell or thought of food, by the arrival of food in the stomach, and by hormones.

Digestive glands in the stomach wall release acid, which assists in digestion and kills off most harmful bacteria. Other glands produce a layer of mucus, which protects your stomach wall from being burned by the acid. If too much acid is produced, it can make a hole in the stomach wall, called an ulcer.

Stomach juices contain enzymes to break down the complex chemicals in food into simpler units.

Three Layers of Muscles

Your stomach is important in the mechanical churning of your food. Because it has three layers of muscles, contracting in different directions, your stomach can mash your food thoroughly and mix it with digestive juices.

The result is a soupy paste. Then your stomach muscles move the food toward the next part of your alimentary canal, the duodenum.

Carbohydrate foods are usually the first to move out of your stomach into your duodenum. Proteins and fats, which are more difficult to digest, remain longer in your stomach.

There is a sphincter muscle between your stomach and your duodenum. When it opens briefly, your stomach squeezes out a small amount of food — something like the squeezing of toothpaste out of its tube.

When the sphincter closes, the rest of the food remains in your stomach until the duodenum is ready to receive it.

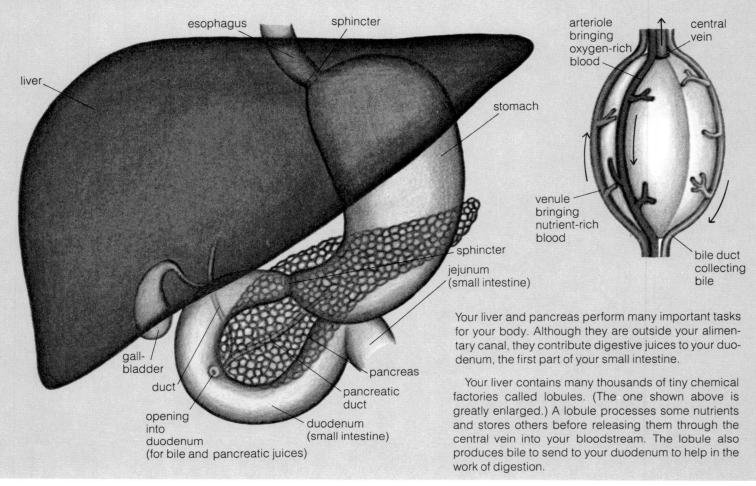

esophagus
sphincter
liver
stomach
arteriole bringing oxygen-rich blood
central vein
venule bringing nutrient-rich blood
sphincter
jejunum (small intestine)
bile duct collecting bile
gall-bladder
duct
pancreas
pancreatic duct
opening into duodenum (for bile and pancreatic juices)
duodenum (small intestine)

Your liver and pancreas perform many important tasks for your body. Although they are outside your alimentary canal, they contribute digestive juices to your duodenum, the first part of your small intestine.

Your liver contains many thousands of tiny chemical factories called lobules. (The one shown above is greatly enlarged.) A lobule processes some nutrients and stores others before releasing them through the central vein into your bloodstream. The lobule also produces bile to send to your duodenum to help in the work of digestion.

Your Small Intestine

Extending from the stomach to the large intestine, the small intestine is the longest part of your alimentary canal. In an average adult it is about 21 feet (6.4 meters) long. It is coiled and folded so as to fit compactly into the abdomen. The first section of the small intestine, the duodenum, is a C-shaped segment about a foot long. The middle section is called the jejunum, and the final section the ileum.

The duodenum receives digestive juices from the pancreas and the liver. The pancreas is like a giant salivary gland. Every day it pours one to two pints (one half to one liter) of digestive juices into the duodenum. These juices contain enzymes that complete the digestion of most carbohydrates into their sugar subunits, which will later be converted into glucose by the liver. Other pancreatic enzymes continue the digestion of proteins and fats.

The liver produces a thick green fluid called bile, which assists in the digestion of fats by making them dissolve in water. Bile is stored in the gallbladder until it is needed by the duodenum.

When you eat a fatty meal, your liver prepares for the extra fat by filling the gallbladder with extra bile. Gallstones may form in the gallbladder from minerals in the bile.

Absorbing the Nutrients

The duodenum passes the partly digested food along to the other two sections of the small intestine. They produce additional digestive juices from millions of glands in their walls — about five pints (2.1 liters) a day.

When the food has finally been broken down into its basic components (amino acids, simple sugars, and fatty acids), they are small enough to be absorbed into the bloodstream. Because of the large quantity of nutrients to be absorbed, this is not an easy task. The

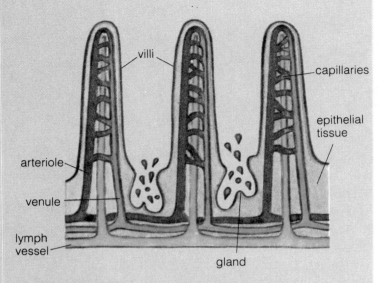

villi

capillaries

epithelial tissue

arteriole

venule

lymph vessel

gland

YOUR SMALL INTESTINE
In the lining of your small intestine are glands that produce mucus and digestive enzymes. The lining, made of epithelial tissue, is folded and refolded to provide a large surface area. Tiny hairlike villi pick up nutrients passing by. Your small intestine is where nutrients move out of your alimentary canal, to be carried to all parts of your body. Carbohydrate and protein nutrients move through the thin walls of your villi into the blood flowing through capillaries. Fat nutrients move through the walls of the villi into lymph vessels.

Your Liver: Complex Organ

The liver is the body's largest internal organ, weighing three to four pounds in an adult. It receives its supply of blood from two sources. About one-fifth is oxygen-rich blood from your heart, and the other four-fifths is nutrient-rich blood from your small intestine. The liver processes some of the nutrients, such as amino acids, in order to meet the special needs of individual tissues elsewhere in your body. The liver stores certain nutrients, such as vitamins, releasing them into the blood when they are required by the body.

Your liver also stores carbohydrates in the form of glycogen. Glycogen can be converted promptly into glucose if glucose is needed for energy by the brain, muscles, or other organs. The brain, which cannot store glucose, depends on a steady supply from the liver.

The formation of glycogen is switched on by a hormone, insulin, which is poured into the blood by the pancreas. An inability to produce insulin leads to diabetes, a disease involving excessive glucose in the blood.

In addition to assisting in digestion, the liver serves many other needs of the body. For example, it breaks down old red blood cells. It also processes potential poisons for removal from the body. These include alcohol (which the liver can process in small amounts) and drugs that have served their purpose.

The Large Intestine

Unlike animals such as cows and horses, human beings are unable to digest cellulose, the fibrous carbohydrate in grass and other plant foods. According to some experts, the appendix (which serves no purpose in human beings) may have been useful to primitive ancestors who needed to digest dense fiber such as bark.

Indigestible parts of food move from the small intestine into the large intestine. There water and needed chemicals are absorbed back into the bloodstream for recycling. The remaining waste travels on to the rectum, ready to pass out of the body through the anus.

Dietary fiber, or roughage, aids in the process of peristalsis and prevents constipation. Good sources of dietary fiber are fresh vegetables, fruits, whole-grain bread, and cereals.

average adult absorbs 10 quarts (about 10 liters) of digested foods and liquids every day.

If the lining of the small intestine were smooth, it would not provide enough surface area to do the job. As a result, the walls of the small intestine are folded and refolded countless times. They are lined with millions of tiny fingerlike projections called villi. The villi wave back and forth, capturing nutrients from the soupy paste passing through the small intestine.

Within each villus is a network of capillaries. In a villus there is also a larger vessel connected to the lymphatic system, another system through which fluids circulate. Amino acids and simple sugars such as glucose pass through the walls of the villi and into the capillaries. Fat nutrients pass through into the lymph vessels. Vitamins and minerals pass unchanged from the small intestine into the blood or lymph. Many of the absorbed nutrients then travel in the bloodstream to the liver.

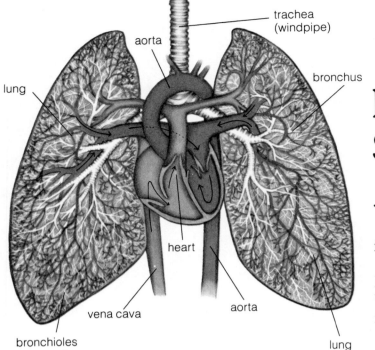

lung

aorta

trachea
(windpipe)

bronchus

heart

vena cava

aorta

bronchioles

lung

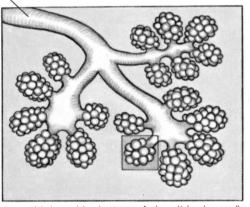

bronchioles with clusters of alveoli (*enlarged*)

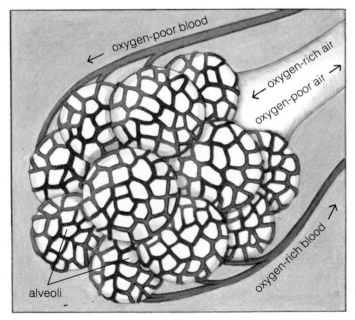

oxygen-poor blood

oxygen-rich air

oxygen-poor air

oxygen-rich blood

alveoli

cluster of alveoli (*further enlarged*)
with network of capillaries

Respiratory System

Y OUR RESPIRATORY SYSTEM supplies oxygen to your body. The oxygen enables your body to burn its fuel — the nutrients in the food you eat.

Oxygen makes up about a fifth of the air around us. By the process of breathing, or respiration, your body brings air into your lungs. There some of the oxygen moves from the air into your bloodstream. At the same time a waste gas, carbon dioxide, moves from your blood into the air, to be breathed out. This process is known as the exchange of gases.

The Heart-Lung Team

When you breathe in, air passages carry oxygen to your lungs. When you breathe out, the air passages carry carbon dioxide away from your lungs.

The lungs work very closely with the heart. By following the arrows in the red passageways in the top drawing at the left, you can trace the path of oxygen-rich blood from the lungs to the left side of the heart. There it is pumped through the largest artery, the aorta, to all parts of the body.

By following the arrows in the blue passageways, you can trace the path of oxygen-poor blood (blood carrying carbon dioxide) into the right side of the heart. There it is pumped to the lungs for the exchange of gases.

The Exchange of Gases

Oxygen and carbon dioxide are exchanged in tiny air sacs, the alveoli. They are in direct contact with capillaries carrying blood. The walls of the air sacs and the capillaries are moist and very thin — much thinner than tissue paper.

Oxygen molecules seep from the alveoli through the thin walls, or membranes, into the blood of your capillaries. The hemoglobin in your red cells picks up the oxygen. At the same time your blood plasma gives up carbon dioxide to the air in the alveoli.

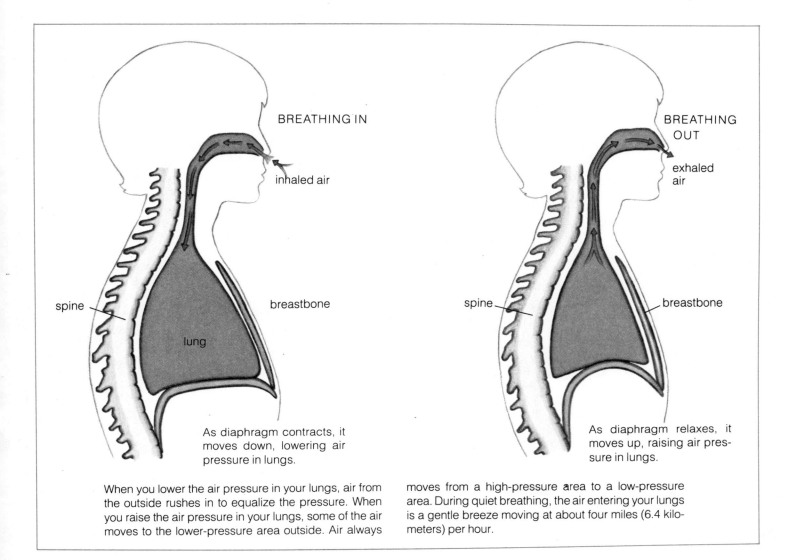

BREATHING IN

inhaled air

spine

breastbone

lung

As diaphragm contracts, it moves down, lowering air pressure in lungs.

When you lower the air pressure in your lungs, air from the outside rushes in to equalize the pressure. When you raise the air pressure in your lungs, some of the air moves to the lower-pressure area outside. Air always

BREATHING OUT

exhaled air

spine

breastbone

As diaphragm relaxes, it moves up, raising air pressure in lungs.

moves from a high-pressure area to a low-pressure area. During quiet breathing, the air entering your lungs is a gentle breeze moving at about four miles (6.4 kilometers) per hour.

How You Breathe

You usually breathe automatically, even if you are unconscious. Since you started reading this chapter you may have taken 10 to 20 breaths without noticing them. In quiet breathing the average adult inhales and exhales about 15 times a minute — perhaps 20,000 times a day.

Your two lungs reach from just above your collarbone down to your diaphragm. They are soft, spongy, very elastic, and light, weighing not much more than a pound (454 grams) each. Surrounding each lung is an airtight covering, the pleura.

An adult's lungs hold three quarts (about three liters) of air. In quiet breathing about a pint (one-half liter) of air is inhaled or exhaled with each breath. But in vigorous exercise four quarts (about four liters) of air may be breathed in and out.

Inhaled air contains about 21 percent oxygen and exhaled air about 16 percent. An office worker may inhale and exhale 3,000 gallons (11,352 liters) of air a day. From this air, the person absorbs 150 gallons (570 liters) of oxygen.

Your lungs have no muscles of their own. The muscles around your chest cavity do the work of breathing.

Your diaphragm does most of the work. This sheet of muscle, stretching from your backbone to the front of your rib cage, makes a movable floor for your lungs. In quiet breathing it moves less than an inch. But during vigorous exercise it can move several inches up and down.

Smaller muscles between your ribs may help to enlarge your chest cavity upward and outward, especially when you take a deep breath.

THE BRONCHIAL TREE

Your trachea (windpipe) branches into two main bronchi, which divide and subdivide into smaller bronchial passages. The smallest air passages are the bronchioles (about 1/50 inch wide), which reach your tiny air sacs, the alveoli. In the lungs of an adult there are about a quarter of a million bronchioles. Your air passages resemble a tree, upside down, with the trunk dividing into smaller branches and then twigs. Like your lungs, a plant's leaves exchange gases. But plants absorb carbon dioxide and expel oxygen, and so they make good partners for human beings.

Your thyroid cartilage protects your voice box (larynx), which contains your vocal cords. The cords, which are usually relaxed and open, tighten when you speak or sing. As your lungs push air up and out, your vocal cords vibrate, making sound waves, which are heard as speech, song, or noise.

Your trachea and your bronchi are held open by C-shaped hoops of cartilage, which do not meet at the back. You can feel some hoops of your trachea at the notch above your breastbone.

THE RESPIRATORY CENTER

The purpose of respiration is the exchange of gases in your lungs. Your respiratory center, in your brain stem, coordinates all the work of respiration. It instructs your diaphragm how fast to suck air into your lungs. It instructs your heart to beat faster if you need more oxygen. You can control your breathing to some extent. But usually your respiratory center takes care of all the work without your having to think about it.

Your lungs contain hundreds of millions of alveoli. They provide a large area for the exchange of gases, 30 to 50 times as large as the surface of your body. The gases can therefore be exchanged very quickly and in large amounts.

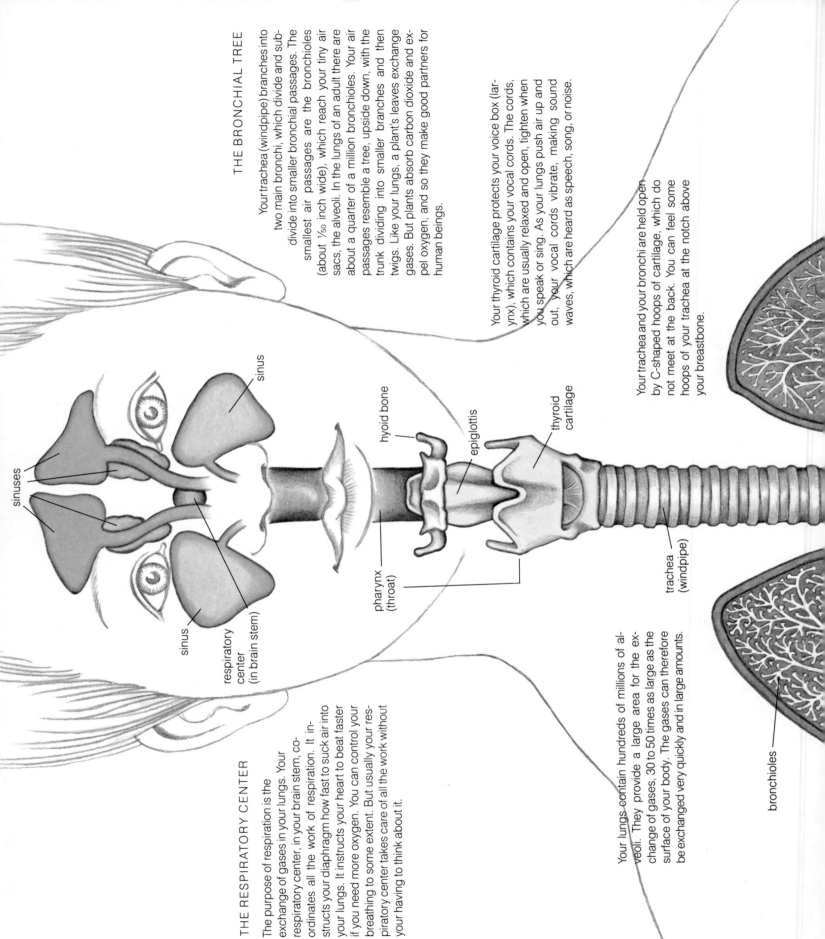

sinus

sinuses

sinus

respiratory center (in brain stem)

hyoid bone

epiglottis

pharynx (throat)

thyroid cartilage

trachea (windpipe)

bronchioles

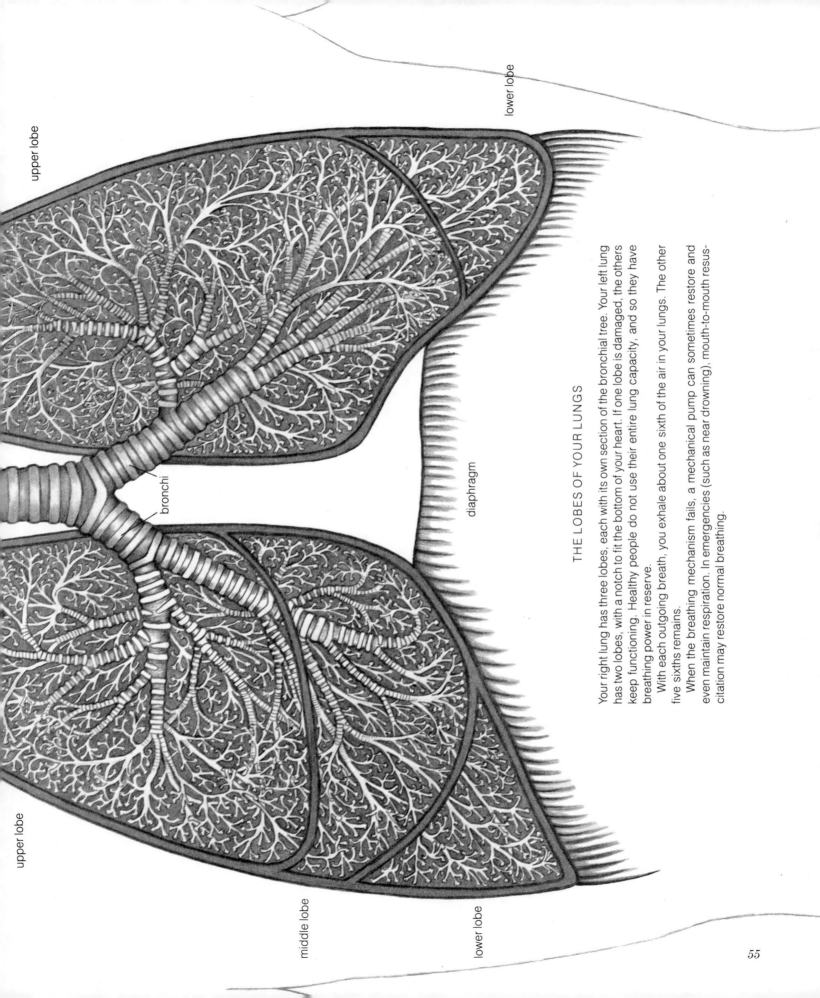

upper lobe

upper lobe

lower lobe

lower lobe

middle lobe

lower lobe

bronchi

diaphragm

THE LOBES OF YOUR LUNGS

Your right lung has three lobes, each with its own section of the bronchial tree. Your left lung has two lobes, with a notch to fit the bottom of your heart. If one lobe is damaged, the others keep functioning. Healthy people do not use their entire lung capacity, and so they have breathing power in reserve.

With each outgoing breath, you exhale about one sixth of the air in your lungs. The other five sixths remains.

When the breathing mechanism fails, a mechanical pump can sometimes restore and even maintain respiration. In emergencies (such as near drowning), mouth-to-mouth resuscitation may restore normal breathing.

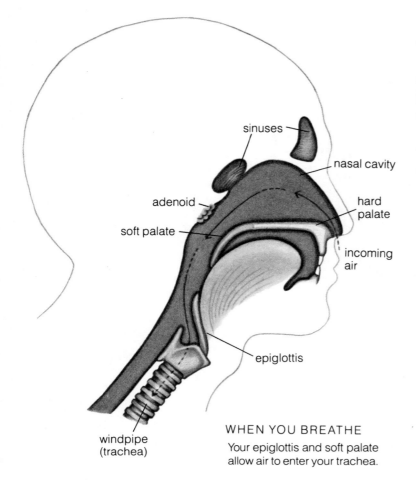

sinuses

nasal cavity

adenoid

hard palate

soft palate

incoming air

epiglottis

windpipe (trachea)

WHEN YOU BREATHE
Your epiglottis and soft palate allow air to enter your trachea.

WHEN YOU SWALLOW
Your epiglottis and soft palate close off your air passages. If you begin to swallow but then stop, you find you cannot breathe.

soft palate

esophagus

food

epiglottis

Like a slow but steady escalator, your cilia can move trapped dirt upward at a rate of nearly one inch per minute. Smoking damages the cilia, so that a smoker's lungs get dirty faster than a nonsmoker's.

wall of air passage

dirt

cilia

mucus

mucous gland

Protecting Your Lungs

The air around us isn't suitable to go directly into our delicate lungs. It is often too dry, usually too cold or too hot, and almost always too dirty. But the respiratory system has several protective devices.

The pharynx (throat) is a passageway for food as well as air. Air entering your food passages does not cause major problems. But food entering the trachea (windpipe) would cause trouble.

So your windpipe has a trapdoor, the epiglottis, which is attached to the root of your tongue. When you swallow, the epiglottis closes over your trachea so that you cannot breathe in food by mistake. Meanwhile, your soft palate closes off the entrance to your nasal cavity.

Very rarely a piece of food gets past the trapdoor into the windpipe. If the choking person cannot speak and grabs his or her throat, doing the Heimlich maneuver may expel the food by compressing the air in the lungs.

If the victim is seated or standing, wrap your arms around the waist from behind. Grasping one fist with your other hand, place it against the abdomen, slightly below the rib cage. Press your fist sharply upward into the abdomen. Repeat if necessary.

If the victim is lying on his or her back, kneel astride the hips, facing the person. With one hand on top of the other, place the heel of your bottom hand on the abdomen slightly below the rib cage. Press hard into the abdomen with a quick upward thrust.

Filtering, Moistening, Warming

Every day you breathe in billions of tiny particles (including dust) that do not belong in your lungs — and some particles not so tiny. Your nose is the first filter for the incoming air. Hairs in your nostrils and bony ridges in your nasal cavity trap the largest particles.

In your nose, throat, and bronchial tree, mucous membranes produce sticky mucus, which traps smaller particles. Tiny hairlike cilia sweep the mucus to your nose and mouth to be swallowed, coughed up, or sneezed or blown out.

Dry incoming air must be humidified. Your nasal cavity is a good humidifier. It gets moisture not only from its own mucus but also from drainage of the sinuses and the tear ducts.

clean lung surface

dirty lung surface

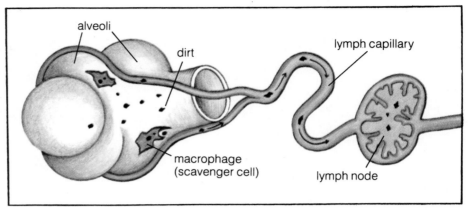

alveoli

dirt

lymph capillary

macrophage
(scavenger cell)

lymph node

PROBLEMS FOR LUNGS
Left: Human lungs are not equipped to cope with all the air pollution of our modern world. *Above:* Your immune system sends white blood cells to your lungs to devour some harmful particles. Others are destroyed in lymph nodes.

Your nose is also a good heater for incoming air. The air is warmed by the blood flowing through the mucous membranes of your nasal cavity. Since air in the alveoli is warmed and saturated with water vapor, your body loses heat and water every time you breathe out. Dogs, because they have very few sweat glands, pant when they are hot to cool down. When you exhale on a cold day, you can see tiny drops of moisture expelled into the cold air with each breath.

Coughing and Sneezing

Coughs and sneezes may seem annoying, but they play an important part in protecting your lungs. In coughing you remove harmful particles or organisms that irritate the lining of your throat, trachea, or bronchial passages.

In sneezing you remove particles or organisms from your nasal cavity. A sneeze is a very strong air current, up to 100 miles (161 kilometers) per hour. If a quiet breath is a gentle breeze, a sneeze is a hurricane.

Help from Your Immune System

The smallest particles in the air can slip through all the filters into your alveoli. These air sacs have no mucus or cilia. Some white cells may destroy the intruders. Other white blood cells carry them through your lymphatic system to nearby lymph nodes to be destroyed. In the sides and roof of your throat, tonsils and adenoids are special lymph organs, which fight harmful bacteria and viruses trapped by the sticky mucus.

Respiratory Diseases

Unfortunately the respiratory system cannot protect the lungs from all the pollution of automobile exhausts, cigarette smoke, and harmful chemicals and gases. A baby's lungs are clean and pink. People who have been smoking for many years, or living in a heavily polluted town, or working in certain kinds of mines or factories have dirty gray lungs with patches of black.

Bacteria or viruses may cause respiratory diseases. The most common of these, of course, is the common cold. A virus gets established in the mucous membrane of your nose and perhaps in that of your throat or sinuses. You may have a runny nose and a sore throat, and you may cough and sneeze.

Like other diseases caused by viruses, the common cold cannot be cured by drugs. But your immune system goes into action against the invaders. Your cold usually disappears within a week or so.

In bronchitis the linings of the air passages swell up. In asthma the bronchial muscles contract, preventing a free flow of air.

Early in this century the two worst killers were respiratory diseases. In tuberculosis, bacteria destroy lung tissue. In pneumonia, the air sacs fill with a sticky material. In both cases not enough oxygen can get into the bloodstream. Fortunately modern drugs can usually prevent or cure these respiratory diseases.

Circulatory System

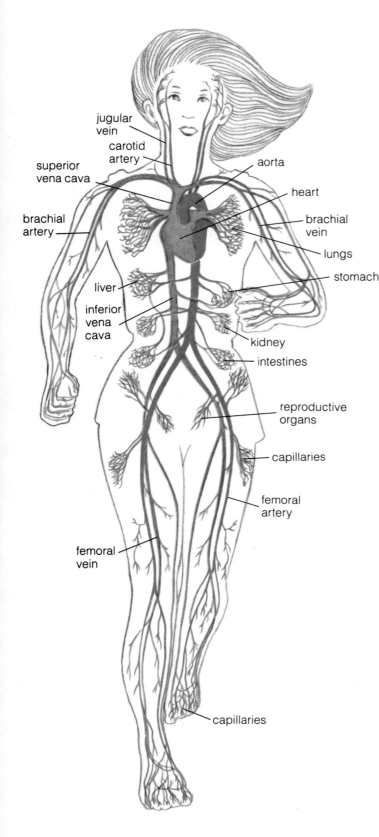

jugular vein
carotid artery
superior vena cava
brachial artery
liver
inferior vena cava
aorta
heart
brachial vein
lungs
stomach
kidney
intestines
reproductive organs
capillaries
femoral artery
femoral vein
capillaries

YOUR CIRCULATORY SYSTEM has two important jobs: transportation of materials and regulation of temperature.

Transportation Network for Your Body

Your heart pumps blood through a system of vessels to all parts of the body. The blood carries nutrients, oxygen, antibodies, and hormones to the cells of your body. The blood also carries waste products away from the cells to disposal sites such as your liver, lungs, and kidneys.

If the blood flow to any part of the body is cut off, that part will quickly die. Brain cells will die after three or four minutes without a fresh supply of blood.

Temperature Control for Your Body

Human beings are warm-blooded animals, with a fairly steady body temperature. Your circulatory system is partly responsible for regulating your temperature.

Warmer blood from the center of your body is brought to the surface to be cooled. On a cold day your skin appears pale, or even blue, because the tiny blood vessels in your skin have contracted and very little blood is flowing through them. This cuts down on the loss of heat through your skin. In hot weather the blood vessels in your skin widen, allowing more blood to flow through them and increasing the loss of heat. Thus your skin looks pinker and feels warmer.

All this work is done by about three to six quarts (three to six liters) of blood, depending on adult body size.

PIPELINES FOR YOUR BLOOD
Throughout your body, thousands of miles of blood vessels run to every living organ and tissue except the cornea of the eye. This drawing includes only a few of the major blood vessels. Arteries (*shown in red*) carry oxygen-rich blood away from your lungs and heart. Veins (*shown in blue*) carry oxygen-poor blood back to your heart and lungs.

In all parts of your body, tiny capillaries connect the smallest arteries with the smallest veins. The capillaries deliver oxygen to every cell of your body and pick up a waste gas, carbon dioxide. As oxygen is used up, the blood turns color, from bright red to dark red.

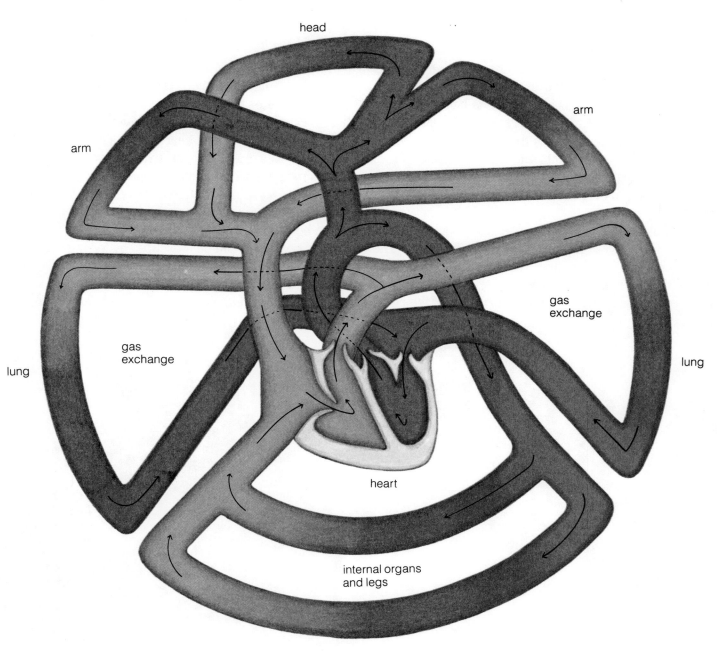

head

arm

arm

gas
exchange

gas
exchange

lung

lung

heart

internal organs
and legs

ROUND TRIPS FOR YOUR BLOOD

Your blood circulates in a closed system, as represented by this circular diagram. Your heart is a pump that keeps your blood moving constantly: away from your heart and lungs, and then back again.

The right side of your heart pumps oxygen-poor blood to your lungs to pick up oxygen. The left side of your heart pumps oxygen-rich blood downward to your legs and internal organs, and upward to your head and arms.

Your Heart

Your heart is in your chest cavity, nestled between your lungs and protected by your breastbone and ribs. The bottom of your heart rests on your diaphragm.

The heart is a very strong and specialized muscle, about the size of a person's fist. In an average adult it weighs 10 to 11 ounces (about 300 grams).

The job of the heart is to pump enough blood at a high enough pressure so that the blood constantly circulates, reaching every part of the body. The heart pumps about 1,250 gallons (4,730 liters) daily.

Your heart contains four chambers. Two of the chambers receive incoming blood. The other two chambers pump blood out of your heart.

Your Heart Chambers

Your heart contains four chambers. When blood is pumped out of the chambers, valves snap shut with a "thump-thump," which is known as the heart sound.

Veins bring blood to the heart from all parts of the body. This blood first enters the right atrium. Then it passes through a valve into the right ventricle. From there it passes through a second valve to the pulmonary artery leading to the lungs. In the lungs, the blood picks up oxygen.

The pulmonary veins bring the blood back from the lungs to the heart, where it enters the left atrium. The blood passes through a third valve to the left ventricle. There the blood is pumped at high pressure through a fourth valve into the aorta, the main artery of the body.

Your Heart Rate

The heart of the average adult beats between 60 and 80 times a minute. Children's heart rates are higher. Trained athletes have slower heart rates because their hearts can pump more blood with every beat.

During exercise your heart rate increases in order to supply your muscles with extra blood. During and after a meal your heart rate increases in order to send extra blood to your digestive organs. When you have a fever, your heart pumps more blood toward the surface of the body to release heat and cool you off.

Your heart rate can be measured by feeling the pulse in the radial artery of your wrist. To feel your pulse, place two fingertips of one hand on the underside of your other wrist just below the base of your thumb.

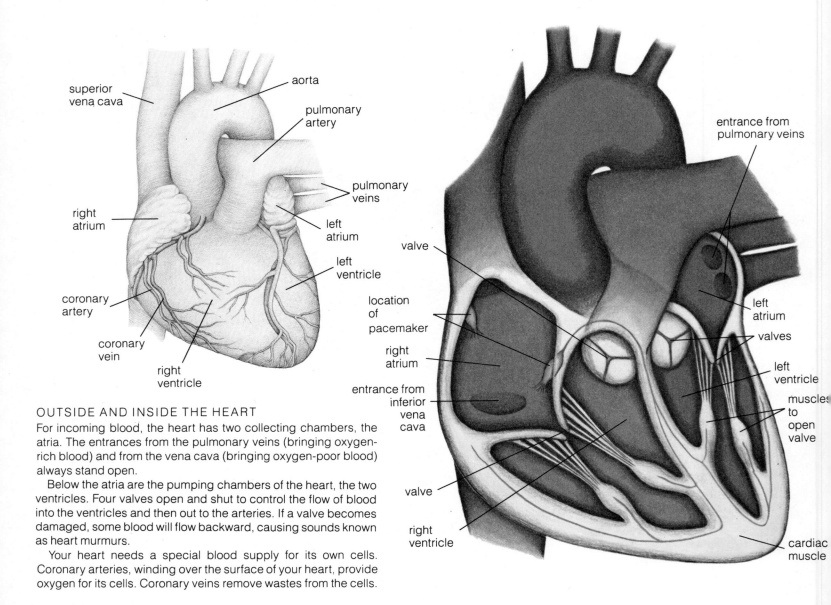

OUTSIDE AND INSIDE THE HEART

For incoming blood, the heart has two collecting chambers, the atria. The entrances from the pulmonary veins (bringing oxygen-rich blood) and from the vena cava (bringing oxygen-poor blood) always stand open.

Below the atria are the pumping chambers of the heart, the two ventricles. Four valves open and shut to control the flow of blood into the ventricles and then out to the arteries. If a valve becomes damaged, some blood will flow backward, causing sounds known as heart murmurs.

Your heart needs a special blood supply for its own cells. Coronary arteries, winding over the surface of your heart, provide oxygen for its cells. Coronary veins remove wastes from the cells.

HOW YOUR HEART BEATS

The muscular contraction of your heart obeys commands from your pacemaker, which consists of specialized tissue within the heart muscle. Its activity may be recorded on an electrocardiogram (EKG). If a person's natural pacemaker fails, it may be replaced by an artificial one.

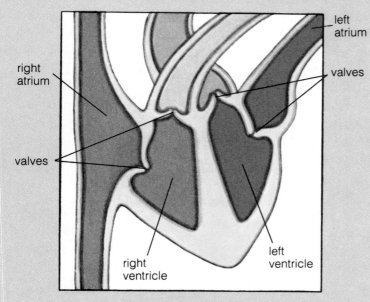

(1) Your two ventricles are full of blood. All four valves are closed. Your atria are beginning to collect more blood.

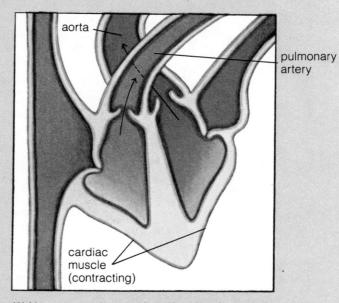

(2) Your pacemaker sends a signal to the muscle tissue of your heart wall. The ventricles contract, pushing open the valves to the aorta and pulmonary artery. The contraction pumps blood.

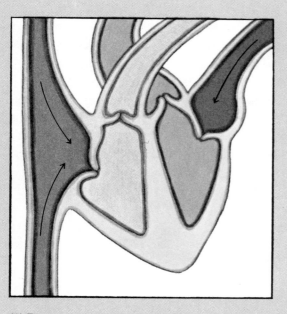

(3) The two valves from the ventricles to the aorta and the pulmonary artery snap shut with a thump. (This can be heard through a stethoscope.) Your ventricles relax. The valves between the atria and the ventricles are still closed. Both atria fill with blood.

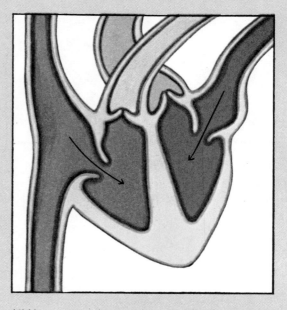

(4) Your pacemaker sends a signal to the muscles that open the valves between the atria and the ventricles. The ventricles fill with blood. The valves snap shut with a second thump. (This too can be heard through a stethoscope.)

The complete cycle of a heartbeat usually takes less than one second. Now your heart is ready for the next heartbeat.

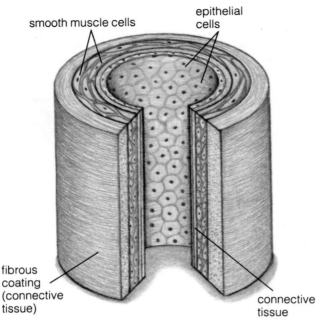

WHAT BLOOD VESSELS ARE MADE OF

Arteries and veins contain three layers of tissue. The inner layer is a smooth lining made of epithelial cells. The middle layer of arteries consists of muscles and, in larger arteries, of elastic tissue. Veins have a very thin middle layer of muscles. An outer layer of connective tissue covers both arteries and veins.

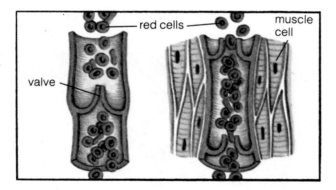

BLOOD FIGHTING GRAVITY

The blood in many of your veins must struggle against gravity to move back up to your heart. With only weak muscles of their own, the veins depend on muscular action and nearby arteries to keep the blood moving. Your veins also have one-way valves.

BLOOD VESSELS LARGE AND SMALL

The largest artery (aorta) and the two largest veins (superior and inferior vena cava) measure about an inch wide. Because of their muscle tissue, the walls of arteries are thicker and firmer than those of veins. A capillary is much smaller than the dot shown here.

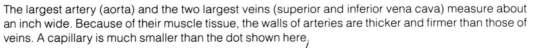
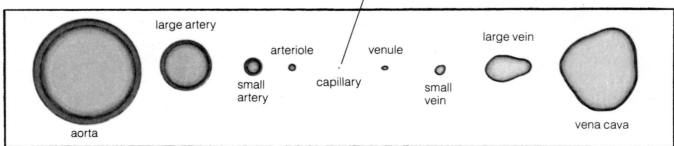

Your Blood Vessels and Blood Pressure

Arteries carry blood away from your heart. They branch like a tree, becoming narrower at each branching. The smallest blood vessels, the capillaries, are barely wide enough to let red cells through. The veins, too, form branching trees. They lead the blood from smaller to larger branches and finally back to the heart.

Healthy blood vessels have smooth, flexible walls. As a person grows older, the walls of the arteries may harden. Their inner surfaces may become rough because of deposits of cholesterol (a fatlike substance) or calcium. This is called hardening of the arteries (arteriosclerosis).

In these narrowed vessels, blood clots are likely to form, clogging an artery. Then the tissues supplied by the artery are deprived of nutrients and oxygen and may die. When this happens in the brain, a stroke will occur. When it happens in the coronary arteries, a part of the heart muscle will die. This is called a heart attack.

Blood pressure is maintained by the pumping action of your heart and by the elasticity of your blood vessels. Blood pressure is usually measured on a person's arm as the blood flows through the brachial artery.

As the artery receives each new spurt of blood, the pressure is highest. This is called systolic pressure. When the heart's ventricles are relaxed, the pressure is lowest. This is called diastolic pressure. The blood pressure is reported as two numbers, for example, 120/80. These numbers mean that the systolic pressure is 120 and the diastolic pressure is 80. (The numbers refer to millimeters of mercury in the tube of the blood-pressure instrument.)

Pressure above 140 systolic or 90 diastolic is usually considered high. It is healthier to have a low blood pressure than a high one. However, if a person's pressure falls too low, there will not be enough blood flowing to the head. If you feel faint, it is best to lower your head by bending over or lying down.

Sometimes a very high pressure will cause a blood vessel to burst. In the brain, a stroke may result not only from a clot but also from a burst blood vessel.

What's in Your Blood

Your blood consists of red cells, white cells, platelets, and plasma, all with specialized jobs. Your red cells carry oxygen to your body cells. Your white cells (discussed on the next page) fight disease. Your platelets help to plug leaks.

Your plasma, which is about 90 percent water, is the liquid part of your blood. Plasma transports the blood cells and platelets, as well as nutrients and hormones. Plasma distributes heat. It also supplies the fluid needed in and around your cells.

Because a mature red cell has no nucleus, it cannot reproduce itself by cell division. So your bone marrow constantly makes new red cells. An adult man has about three trillion red cells, which live for an average of four months. When they are worn out, they are broken up, chiefly in the spleen.

Red cells are flexible enough to squeeze through the tiny capillaries. The red cells pick up oxygen molecules by binding them to a substance called hemoglobin. Iron is an essential part of hemoglobin. As the red cells reach the capillaries they give up their oxygen to the surrounding tissue.

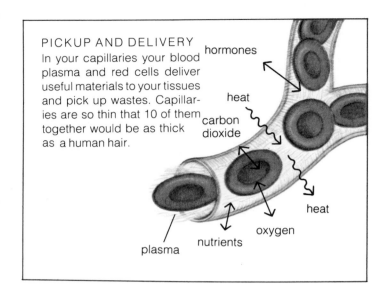

PICKUP AND DELIVERY
In your capillaries your blood plasma and red cells deliver useful materials to your tissues and pick up wastes. Capillaries are so thin that 10 of them together would be as thick as a human hair.

hormones
heat
carbon dioxide
heat
oxygen
nutrients
plasma

Normally red cells make up about 45 percent of the blood volume. When a person does not have enough healthy red cells, the condition is known as anemia.

Platelets are tiny bits broken from big cells in your bone marrow. They live only about four days. Their purpose is to clump together to help form blood clots, which prevent loss of blood. Blood without enough platelets cannot clot, so that even a small cut can be dangerous.

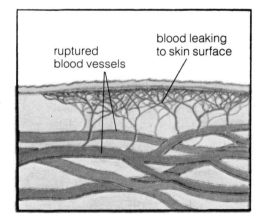

ruptured blood vessels
blood leaking to skin surface

BLACK-AND-BLUE MARK
If you bang your arm or leg against something hard, you may develop a bruise. Under the surface of your skin, blood is leaking from broken blood vessels.

STOPPING LEAKS
(1) A pinprick through your skin may hit a blood vessel. Blood flows out of the vessel into your skin. (2) Small platelets from your blood rush to fill the wound. (3) The platelets help to form a material of sticky threads. The threads make a web that clots the blood and stops the bleeding. (4) Healthy skin cells grow back over the wound. A person whose blood does not clot easily may have the condition known as hemophilia.

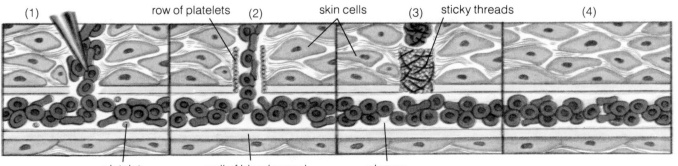

(1)　row of platelets　(2)　skin cells　(3)　sticky threads　(4)

platelet　wall of blood vessel　plasma

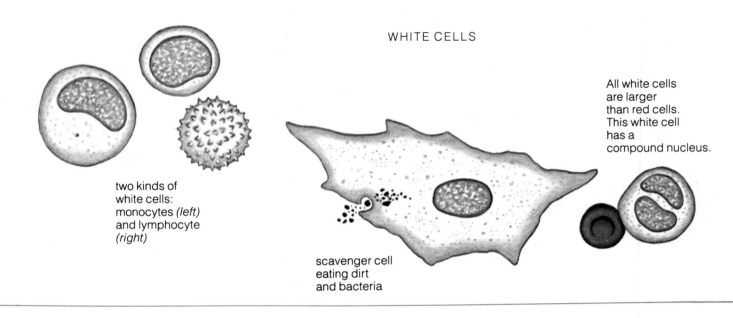

two kinds of
white cells:
monocytes *(left)*
and lymphocyte
(right)

scavenger cell
eating dirt
and bacteria

All white cells
are larger
than red cells.
This white cell
has a
compound nucleus.

Your White Cells

White blood cells are sometimes twice as large as red cells. There is only one white cell for every 500 to 1,000 red cells.

White cells are made not only in your bone marrow but also in your lymph network. White cells glide through the walls of the blood vessels to do their work in the tissues that need them.

When disease organisms (viruses or bacteria) enter the body, more white cells are automatically manufactured in order to fight the infection. Many are scavenger cells. They assist in fighting infections by destroying bacteria and eating them up and by removing wastes and dead cells.

Leukemia results from an uncontrolled production of white cells that remain immature. These useless cells take up so much room in the bloodstream that there is not enough room for healthy red and white cells.

Your Immune System

Bacteria or viruses can attack your body by several routes. They may be floating in the air you breathe. They may enter through a break in your skin or mucous membranes. Or they may arrive in contaminated food or water.

If the attackers take hold, your body can mobilize a counterattack force: your immune system. It works through disease-fighting proteins called antibodies. Your body produces thousands of different kinds of antibodies. It can make many kinds of antibodies against each kind of virus or bacterium.

Antibodies are made in your lymph network. They

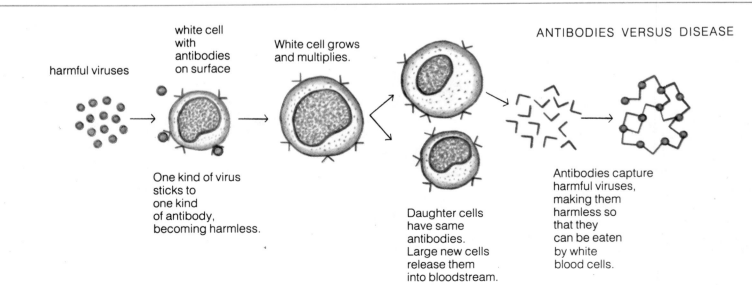

harmful viruses

white cell
with
antibodies
on surface

White cell grows
and multiplies.

One kind of virus
sticks to
one kind
of antibody,
becoming harmless.

Daughter cells
have same
antibodies.
Large new cells
release them
into bloodstream.

Antibodies capture
harmful viruses,
making them
harmless so
that they
can be eaten
by white
blood cells.

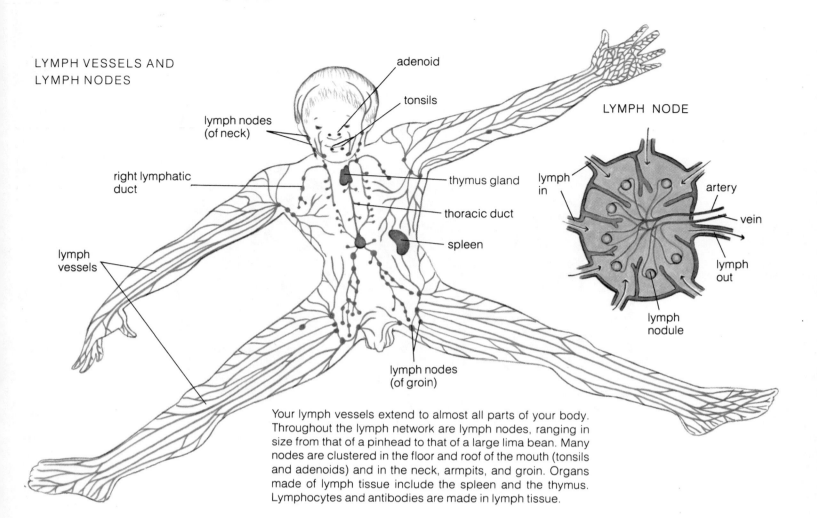

adenoid

tonsils

lymph nodes
(of neck)

right lymphatic
duct

lymph
vessels

thymus gland

thoracic duct

spleen

lymph nodes
(of groin)

LYMPH NODE

lymph
in

artery

vein

lymph
out

lymph
nodule

Your lymph vessels extend to almost all parts of your body. Throughout the lymph network are lymph nodes, ranging in size from that of a pinhead to that of a large lima bean. Many nodes are clustered in the floor and roof of the mouth (tonsils and adenoids) and in the neck, armpits, and groin. Organs made of lymph tissue include the spleen and the thymus. Lymphocytes and antibodies are made in lymph tissue.

are attached to the surface of special white cells, lymphocytes from bone marrow. The lymphocyte, which can "remember" the specific disease organism, divides into more cells. These produce large numbers of free-moving antibodies useful against the same disease. The antibodies seek out all the organisms of that disease and make them harmless.

This process can cure you of a common cold in a week or so. The same process cures you of far more serious diseases. Through inoculation, it can make you immune to such diseases as measles, smallpox, and polio.

Your immune system can also cause trouble for your body. In the case of some allergies, your antibodies wage a vigorous fight against a substance that is harmless to most people.

Your Lymph Network

In addition to its role in your immune system, your lymph network performs other important tasks for your body. The nodes contain scavenger cells that eat and destroy disease organisms. When the nodes are actively fighting infection, they become enlarged and tender. Then you may have a sore throat or infected tonsils. If the nodes and lymph vessels themselves become infected, you are said to have "blood poisoning."

Blood plasma, after leaking out of your capillaries into the spaces between your cells, is called tissue fluid. It is drained back into your bloodstream through either your veins or your lymph network. The lymph fluid empties back into your bloodstream near your left shoulder. Like your veins, your lymph vessels have many valves to prevent backflow.

The thymus gland produces special types of lymphocytes. It is quite large in early childhood, but it becomes small in adulthood. The spleen plays an important role in breaking down worn-out red cells. It also stores red cells. The spleen contracts to release red cells needed elsewhere. This contraction might cause a pain, a "stitch," in the upper left part of your abdomen.

Your lymph network also serves your digestive system by transporting fat nutrients from your small intestine to your cells.

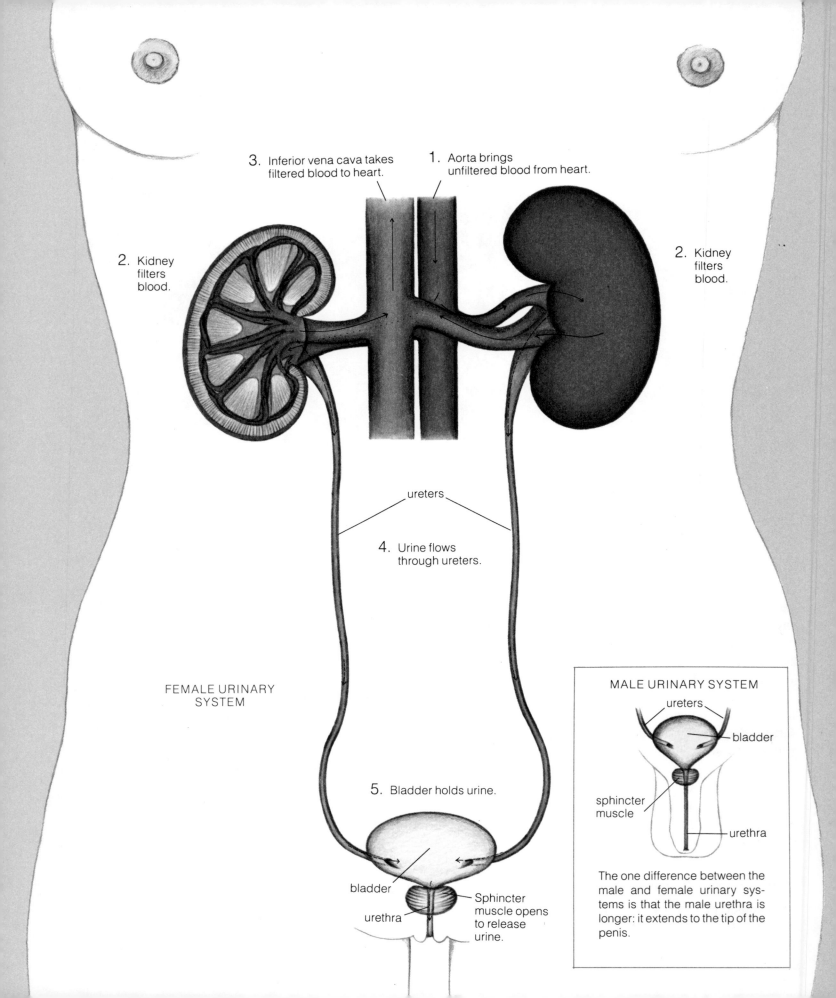

3. Inferior vena cava takes filtered blood to heart.

1. Aorta brings unfiltered blood from heart.

2. Kidney filters blood.

2. Kidney filters blood.

ureters

4. Urine flows through ureters.

FEMALE URINARY SYSTEM

5. Bladder holds urine.

bladder

urethra

Sphincter muscle opens to release urine.

MALE URINARY SYSTEM

ureters

bladder

sphincter muscle

urethra

The one difference between the male and female urinary systems is that the male urethra is longer: it extends to the tip of the penis.

Urinary System

YOUR URINARY SYSTEM has two important jobs. It cleans your blood, and it regulates the amount of water in your body.

Feel the lowest ribs in your back. The kidneys are just inside that part of your rib cage. Each is about five inches long and two inches wide (11 centimeters by 5 centimeters). The artery entering each kidney divides into a network of blood vessels. Each blood vessel ends in a tuft of capillaries called a glomerulus. Each glomerulus is surrounded by the end of a tube, which forms a capsule.

When blood passes through the glomerulus, a certain amount of blood plasma is filtered through its thin walls into the capsule. This fluid is called the filtrate. The amount of filtrate from all the glomeruli is very large, averaging 180 quarts (about 180 liters) per day. The filtrate passes from the capsule through a series of tubes to the entrance of the ureter.

In the tubes the fluid is changed greatly to become urine. Most of the water is returned to the bloodstream. So are most of the substances important to the body, including glucose, amino acids, and salts. Waste products from the liver and other organs are eliminated in the urine. By the time the urine enters the ureters, it has dwindled to 1½ quarts (1.5 liters) a day.

The urine flows down the ureters into your bladder. The bladder is a collapsible bag lying in the front of your pelvis. The bladder wall, containing smooth muscles, is very elastic. When the wall is stretched by a large enough quantity of urine, nerve endings in the wall are stimulated. The nerves send messages to the central nervous system conveying the need to urinate.

The bladder opens into the urethra, a tube that leads outside the body. The opening from the bladder to the urethra is usually kept closed by two sphincter muscles. Movement of the outer sphincter is under voluntary control. When you need to urinate, you can relax the sphincter so that fluid will flow out. You can also suppress this relaxation, at least for a time.

The Salt Water Inside You

Water makes up two thirds of a person's body weight — for example, 100 pounds of water in a 150-pound person. Two thirds of the water is inside the body's

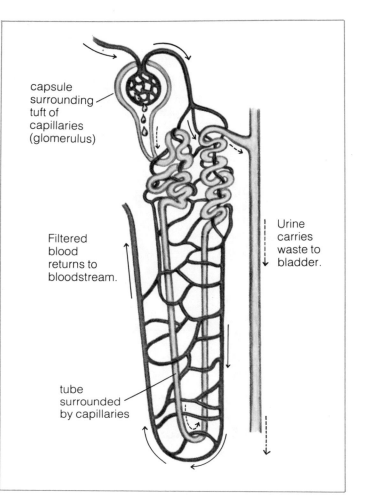

ONE OF YOUR FILTERING UNITS

A kidney has about a million tiny filtering units called nephrons. In the glomerulus and part of the tube system, wastes are removed from the blood. In other parts of the tube system, water and chemicals needed by the body are absorbed back into the blood and recycled.

cells. One third is outside the cells, either in the bloodstream (as plasma) or in body cavities or between the cells (as tissue fluid). Dissolved in the water are various chemicals necessary for the body's work.

The salt content of the body's water is especially important for the survival of its cells. Our inner environment resembles the saltwater environment in which the original single-celled animals lived. If excess salt is present in our tissues, the kidneys eliminate it. If excess water is present, the kidneys eliminate that.

If a person's kidneys are inefficient, a machine that filters blood can do their work. The filtering process is called dialysis. A kidney can also be transplanted. Since a person can easily survive with only one healthy kidney, it is possible to donate a kidney to somebody else.

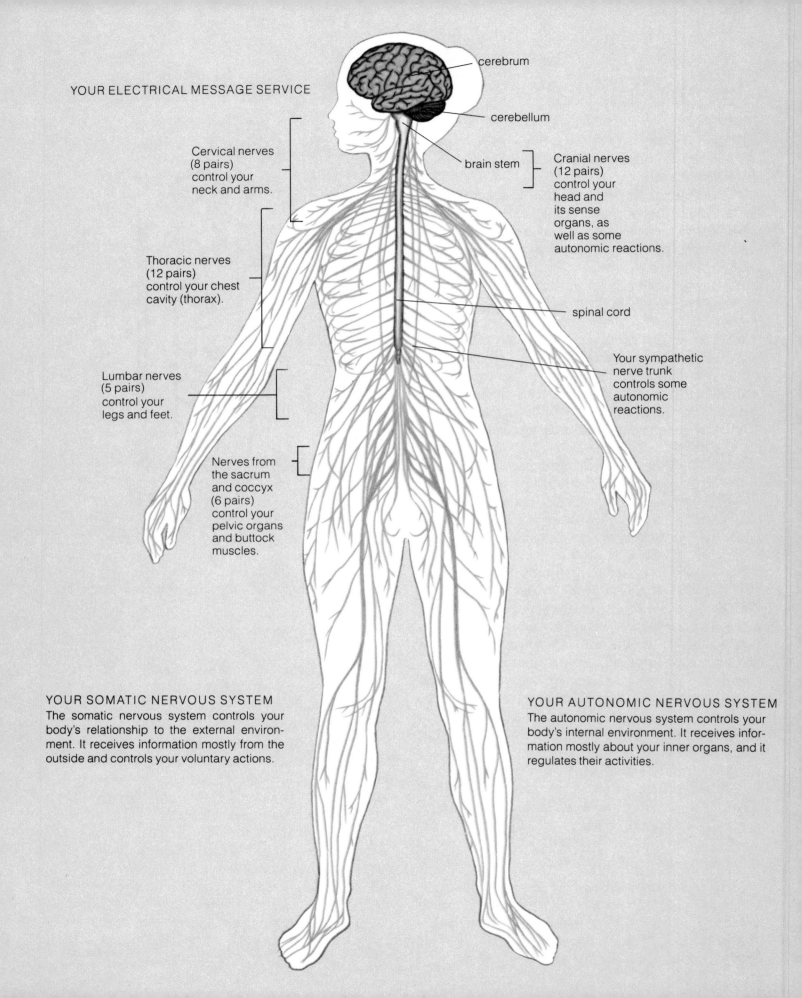

YOUR ELECTRICAL MESSAGE SERVICE

cerebrum

cerebellum

brain stem

Cervical nerves
(8 pairs)
control your
neck and arms.

Cranial nerves
(12 pairs)
control your
head and
its sense
organs, as
well as some
autonomic reactions.

Thoracic nerves
(12 pairs)
control your chest
cavity (thorax).

spinal cord

Lumbar nerves
(5 pairs)
control your
legs and feet.

Your sympathetic
nerve trunk
controls some
autonomic
reactions.

Nerves from
the sacrum
and coccyx
(6 pairs)
control your
pelvic organs
and buttock
muscles.

YOUR SOMATIC NERVOUS SYSTEM
The somatic nervous system controls your
body's relationship to the external environment. It receives information mostly from the
outside and controls your voluntary actions.

YOUR AUTONOMIC NERVOUS SYSTEM
The autonomic nervous system controls your
body's internal environment. It receives information mostly about your inner organs, and it
regulates their activities.

Nervous System

THE NERVOUS SYSTEM controls the actions and sensations of all the parts of your body, as well as your thoughts, emotions, and memories.

Through a complex network of nerves, electrical signals carry messages to and from your brain. Your nervous system is always collecting information from inside and outside your body. The system processes that information, storing some of it and acting on some of it by sending messages to your muscles and internal organs.

For example, as you read this page, your nervous system is performing many different tasks — all with split-second timing and the greatest efficiency. It is directing certain muscles to move your eyes from left to right and back again. Your eyes are sending a steady flow of information to your brain. Recognizing the image of each letter, your brain is combining the letters into words and sentences. Some of the information you are gathering will be stored in your brain as memories. Meanwhile, your brain is recalling some of your old memories to help in understanding new ideas.

At the same time, your nervous system is instructing many of your skeletal muscles to keep you in a sitting position as you hold this book. Other muscles blink your eyes about 25 times a minute.

Your nervous system is also receiving messages from your internal organs. It is sending back messages that control your heart rate, blood pressure, breathing rate, body temperature, digestion of your food, and many other body functions. Through your nervous system, you may realize that you are tired or that dinner is cooking. Your brain knows where you are, about what time it is, and whether you are hungry. And all this is only a small part of the work being done right now by your nervous system.

The Parts of Your Nervous System

Your central nervous system consists of your brain and your spinal cord. Your brain contains the cerebrum, the cerebellum, and the brain stem (discussed on pages 72 and 73). Your spinal cord carries messages between your brain and the lower parts of your body.

Your peripheral (outer) nervous system consists of nerves emerging from your brain (cranial nerves) and others emerging from your spinal cord (spinal nerves). Most peripheral nerves contain two kinds of fibers. The sensory fibers bring messages to the central nervous system from your skin, muscles, and special sense organs such as the eyes. The motor fibers carry instructions from the central nervous system to your skeletal muscles. These form the somatic nervous system, which controls your body's relationship to the world outside itself — the external environment.

Many peripheral nerves also contain fibers leading to and from your internal organs or the glands of your circulatory, digestive, respiratory, and reproductive systems. These nerve fibers belong to the autonomic nervous system. The term "autonomic" refers to activities that are involuntary, or outside your conscious control.

The control center for your autonomic nervous system is in your brain stem and deep in the brain (hypothalamus). The autonomic nervous system works through two sets of nerves, the sympathetic and the parasympathetic nerves. These nerves work closely with the hormones of your endocrine system.

Using Your Brain

You have billions of neurons (nerve cells) in your brain. Since there are so many, an almost infinite number of connections can be made between them. When you learn a new skill, you are training your neurons to connect in a new way. New ideas also come about from new connections between neurons.

Although your body cannot manufacture new neurons, you can establish new connections between the neurons you were born with. The more you use your brain, the more efficient it will become.

Your Nerves

The basic cells of your nervous system are the neurons. These are cells with the special ability to carry and transmit electrical signals.

The number of neurons in a human body has been estimated to be between 10 billion and 100 billion. Most of the neurons are in the brain. Before birth they are formed very rapidly (about 250,000 per minute), but

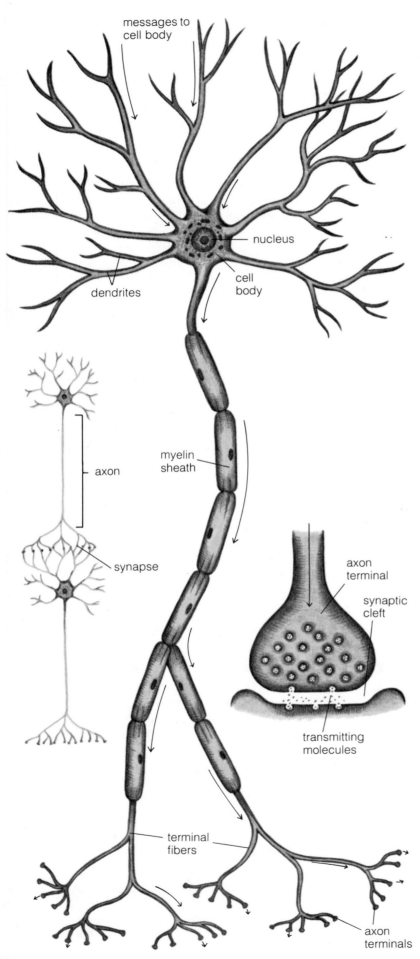

messages to cell body

dendrites

nucleus

cell body

axon

myelin sheath

synapse

axon terminal

synaptic cleft

transmitting molecules

terminal fibers

axon terminals

after birth they stop reproducing. Although damaged neurons can repair themselves to some extent, dead neurons cannot be replaced.

The neuron consists of a cell body, from which branch several dendrites and one axon. The dendrites are short fibers that bring electrical signals to the cell body from sensory receptors or from the axons of many other neurons. The axon is a long fiber that carries the signal away from the cell body to the dendrites of other neurons or to muscles or glands.

Some neurons, especially those in the brain, are very small. Others have very long axons, making them the longest cells in your body. Neurons running from the lower part of your spinal cord to your toes may grow as long as four feet (1.3 meters).

Some nerve fibers are wrapped in a sheath of fatty material called myelin, which is made by special cells surrounding the neurons. Electrical signals can "jump" across gaps in the neurons' sheaths. Myelin-covered fibers are able to carry electrical impulses much faster than uncovered fibers can. The thickest myelin-covered fibers can transmit impulses at a rate of 450 feet (150 meters) per second. The uncovered fibers can manage a speed of only about three feet (one meter) per second.

One neuron does not directly touch another neuron. Messages are passed from one to the next by a chemical process. The point at which the axon of one cell reaches a dendrite of another cell is called a synapse. Between the axon and the dendrite there is a tiny gap called a synaptic cleft.

An electrical signal coming from the cell body of one neuron travels to the end of the axon. There it causes tiny droplets of certain chemicals to be released into the synaptic cleft. The chemicals, called neurotransmitters, travel across the cleft. They are picked up by the end of a dendrite of the next neuron. The dendrite is then stimulated to trans-

TRANSMITTING ELECTRICAL SIGNALS

A neuron's cell body is protected inside your spinal cord or brain. Many short fibers, the dendrites, collect messages for the cell body. One long fiber, the axon, passes the message along to other cells at a junction called the synapse. With the help of chemical transmitters, the message crosses a small gap (the synaptic cleft) from the axon of one cell to a dendrite of another cell. The message crosses the synapse in less than 1/10,000 of a second (100 microseconds).

Your sensory nerves often report information directly to your brain for a decision. In case of an emergency, such as the burning of your fingers by a match, your spinal cord immediately instructs your fingers to drop the match — even before the sensation of pain reaches your brain. The spinal cord is shown here from above, surrounded by the protective bony structure of a neck vertebra.

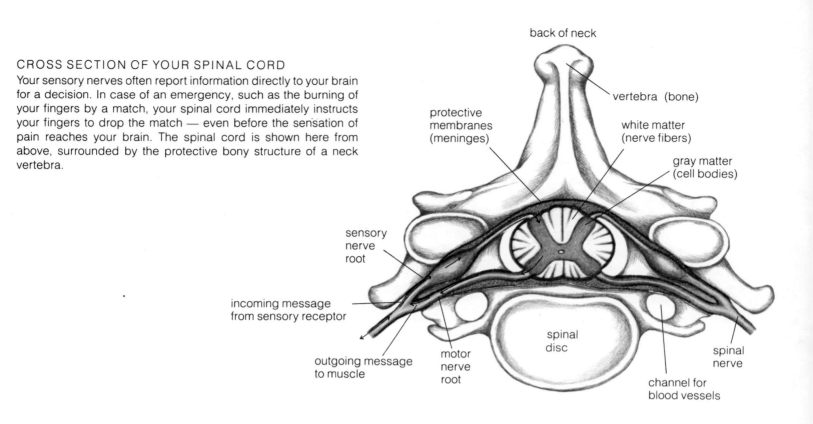

mit an electrical signal of its own. This entire process takes less than 1/10,000 of a second (100 microseconds).

Your Spinal Cord

Your spinal cord reaches from your brain about two thirds of the way down your spinal column. Many nerves branch off from the cord. At the lower end of the cord are nerve fibers that continue to run downward within the spinal canal like the hairs of a horse's tail.

Wrapped around the cord and the brain are three layers of protective membranes called meninges. A fluid derived from the blood plasma fills the space between the two innermost meningeal layers. This is called cerebrospinal fluid. Its main purpose is to protect the central nervous system by acting as a cushion.

When bacteria or viruses invade the area of the meninges, they may spread very rapidly through the cerebrospinal fluid. This condition, known as meningitis, causes a grave threat to the nervous system.

The center of the spinal cord consists of cell bodies arranged in an H-shaped pattern. The arms of the H in back consist of the bodies of sensory nerves, and the arms in front consist of the bodies of motor nerves. Since this H-shaped mass has a grayish hue, it is called the gray matter.

Around the gray matter are nerve fibers coated with fatty (myelinated) sheaths. Since they look shiny and white, they are known as the white matter.

At regular intervals, bunches of these fibers join together and branch outward from the cord to form the spinal nerves. These travel to different parts of the body. There are 31 pairs of spinal nerves, each containing many thousands of sensory and motor nerve fibers.

Reflex Actions

The spinal cord has two main functions. It carries impulses up and down between the brain and other parts of the body. It also serves as a reflex center. Reflexes are automatic responses to stimuli that may not require any communication with the brain.

When a doctor taps your knee in a certain place, it will jerk in a reflex action. This simple reflex involves only two neurons, one sensory and one motor. When you burn your finger, your hand will automatically jerk away from the heat. This too is a simple reflex, occurring even before your brain receives the message of pain traveling up your spinal cord.

Your Brain

The brain is the most complex part of the nervous system. It is surrounded and protected by the bones of the skull, by the meninges, and by the cerebrospinal fluid. The fluid occupies four spaces, called ventricles. It is drained from the ventricles into the space between the meninges, and it eventually returns to the bloodstream. Thus it is constantly being renewed. The discs between the vertebrae provide cushioning for the brain, which rests on top of your spinal column.

Although the brain makes up only 2 percent of the body's weight, it consumes 20 percent of the energy produced. The energy comes from glucose and oxygen brought by the blood. When your blood glucose (blood sugar) level is too low, at first you feel hungry and irritable. Then your brain partly shuts down its operations so that you become weak and faint.

Oxygen is even more urgently needed. Brain cells deprived of oxygen will die in less than five minutes. If the circulation to one part of the brain is shut off, as in a stroke, that area will die.

We can simplify our understanding of the complex brain by dividing it into three parts: the brain stem, the cerebellum, and the cerebrum.

The brain stem is an extension of the spinal cord. Special groups of neurons within the brain stem are called vital centers. They control such involuntary activities as breathing, heart rate, and blood pressure.

The main functions of the cerebellum concern physical coordination. It orchestrates the movements of your muscles so that they are smooth and synchronized. The cerebellum receives sensory input from the organs of balance of the inner ears and from joints and muscles. It plays an important part in maintaining balance and equilibrium.

Your Cerebrum

The largest and most sophisticated part of your brain is the cerebrum. Its two huge hemispheres are joined by several bands of nerve fibers, including the corpus callosum. Each hemisphere consists of a core of white matter (myelin-covered nerve fibers) surrounded by a layer of gray matter called the cerebral cortex. It is the cerebral cortex that starts and stops all your voluntary movements. It receives all your conscious body sensations. And it is responsible for learning, judgment, creativity, and some of your emotions.

Different parts of the cortex are responsible for different functions. For example, the "motor strip" on each hemisphere controls voluntary movements. Such movements of each side of the body are controlled by the cortex of the opposite side of the brain. Sensations such as pain, heat or cold, pressure, or a pinprick are also received by the opposite side of the brain. Special sensations such as sight, hearing, taste, and smell are received by other areas of the cortex. For example, the visual cortex at the back of your skull receives messages from your eyes.

Most people depend more on the left hemisphere of their brain than on the right. That is why most people are right-handed. The left hemisphere in most right-handed people (and some left-handed people) is responsible for producing and understanding speech, reading, writing, and logical thinking. The right hemisphere is more important in the perception of music, artistic ability, creativity, and the emotions.

When we sleep, the entire cortex functions at a slower rate than when we are awake. Diseases or damage affecting the cerebral cortex as a whole will cause a clouding or a loss of consciousness. Certain drugs can also cause the same problems.

Damage to a specific part of the cortex, as in a stroke, will result in a loss of function associated with that part. Therefore, a stroke in the motor area of the left hemisphere will paralyze all or part of the right side of the body and may cause a loss of the ability to speak.

Sometimes, however, an injury of the brain will result in an area of irritation that causes the neurons to be hyperactive. In such cases there may be violent, uncontrolled movements in the part of the body controlled by the injured part of the brain. This is the cause of epilepsy.

Some areas deep in the brain are known to be associated with memory, but the mechanics of memory are still not fully understood. We do know that there are two types of memory, short term and long term.

Connections of neurons are important in making the associations that recall memories. If certain associations are made over and over again, they become like well-worn paths in your brain. Memory can probably be improved by regular use.

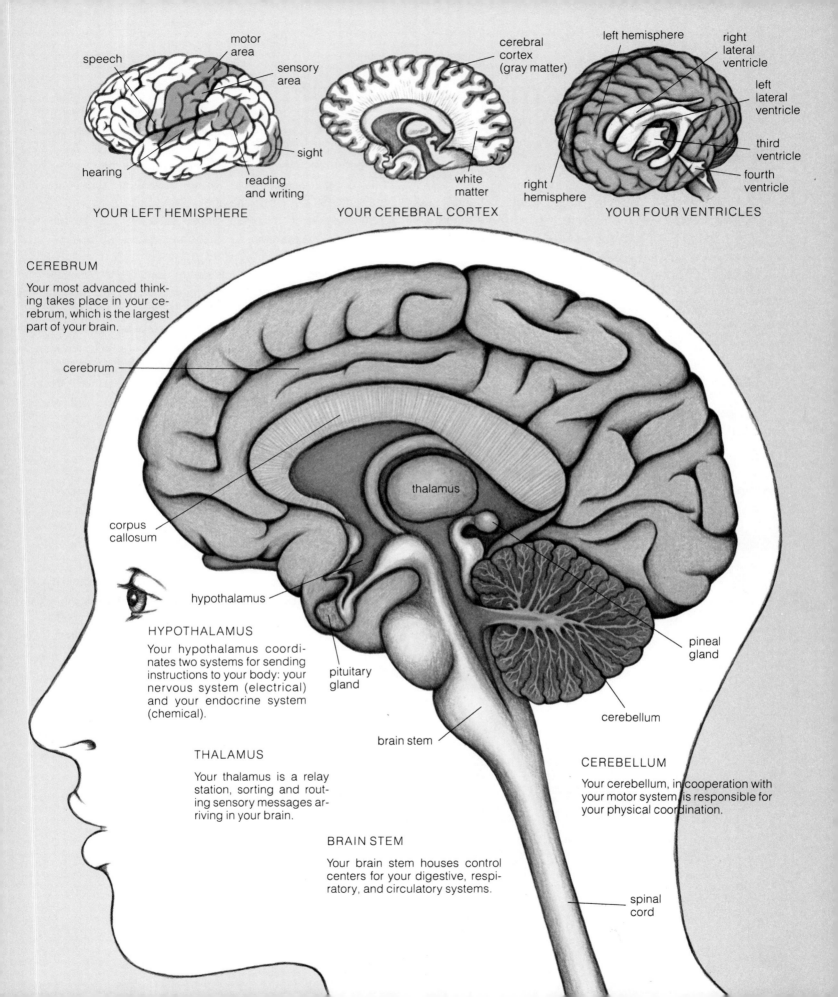

speech

motor area

sensory area

sight

hearing

reading and writing

YOUR LEFT HEMISPHERE

cerebral cortex (gray matter)

white matter

YOUR CEREBRAL CORTEX

left hemisphere

right lateral ventricle

left lateral ventricle

third ventricle

fourth ventricle

right hemisphere

YOUR FOUR VENTRICLES

CEREBRUM

Your most advanced thinking takes place in your cerebrum, which is the largest part of your brain.

cerebrum

thalamus

corpus callosum

hypothalamus

pineal gland

HYPOTHALAMUS

Your hypothalamus coordinates two systems for sending instructions to your body: your nervous system (electrical) and your endocrine system (chemical).

pituitary gland

cerebellum

brain stem

THALAMUS

Your thalamus is a relay station, sorting and routing sensory messages arriving in your brain.

CEREBELLUM

Your cerebellum, in cooperation with your motor system, is responsible for your physical coordination.

BRAIN STEM

Your brain stem houses control centers for your digestive, respiratory, and circulatory systems.

spinal cord

Sensory Systems

HOW DOES YOUR brain get information from outside your body? Your ears, eyes, and other sense organs collect this information.

A sense organ contains many double-ended cells called receptor cells. The outer end collects information in the form of light rays, sound waves, or pressure — or even tiny food molecules floating in the air. The receptor cell converts this information into electrical signals.

From the inner end of the receptor cell, sensory nerves carry the electrical signals to special areas of your brain. Your brain converts the electrical signals into sights or sounds, smells or tastes, pressures or pain.

Your Nose

The sense of smell developed many millions of years ago in very primitive forms of life. Some insects can locate mates many miles away by smell alone. Compared to many other animals, human beings have a rather poor sense of smell.

Odors are chemical particles floating in the air. The receptor cells that react to odors are in the upper half of each nostril and within the nasal cavity. The receptor cells occupy an area about the size of a postage stamp.

The receptor cells for odors, called olfactory rods, have little hairs that lie bathed in mucus. Odors become absorbed in the mucus, where they come in contact with the olfactory rods. The olfactory rods send electrical signals to the nerve cells in the olfactory bulb, which is just above the roof of the nasal cavity and is protected by a sievelike plate of bone. From the olfactory bulb, messages go to a special area of your cerebral cortex. There your brain perceives different smells as distinct from one another.

Stimulation of the brain by certain odors may result in automatic responses from the nervous system. For example, pleasant food odors may stimulate the production of saliva or gastric juices in your digestive system. Disagreeable odors may cause gagging or even vomiting. Your sense of smell can alert you to airborne signals of danger such as smoke or poisonous gases — or even skunks. And it can help your taste buds to warn you not to consume spoiled foods or liquids.

When you breathe normally, only a small amount of an odor may reach the olfactory rods. If you want to identify it, you will probably sniff. Sniffing brings more of the odor to your olfactory rods.

Your Tongue

Certain chemicals from your food become dissolved in the saliva of your mouth. When receptor cells in the taste buds of your tongue and mouth come in contact with those chemicals, you experience the sensation of taste.

Each taste bud is a small, round collection of receptor cells. You have many taste buds on the tip and the root of your tongue, and others on the soft part of your palate. It is sometimes said that there are four basic

HOW A RECEPTOR CELL SERVES YOUR BRAIN
A receptor cell collects information and converts it into electrical signals to pass along to your brain.

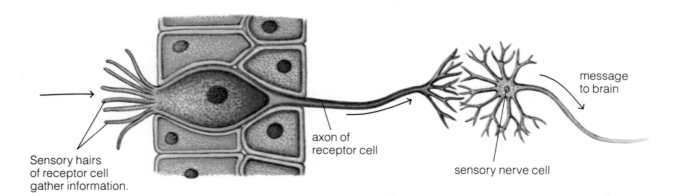

Sensory hairs of receptor cell gather information.

axon of receptor cell

sensory nerve cell

message to brain

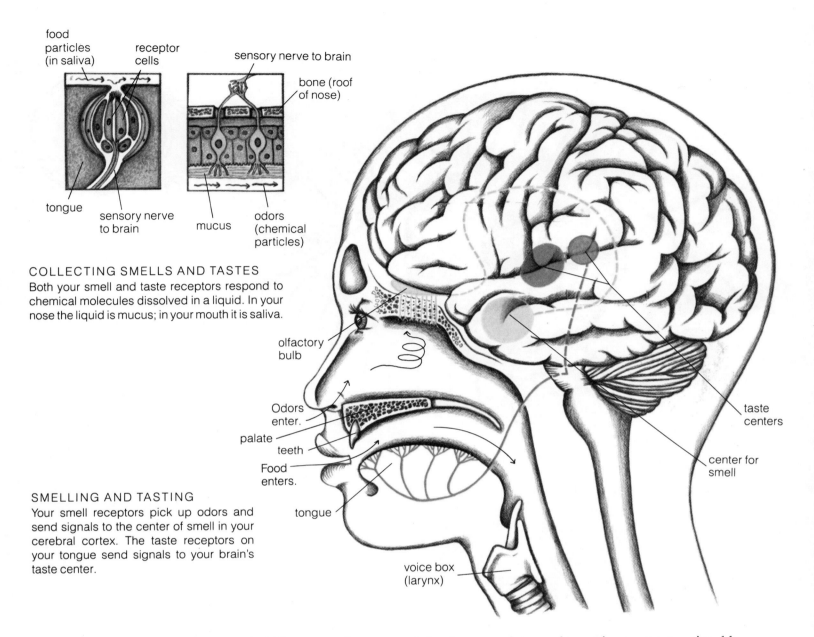

food particles (in saliva)

receptor cells

sensory nerve to brain

bone (roof of nose)

tongue

sensory nerve to brain

mucus

odors (chemical particles)

COLLECTING SMELLS AND TASTES
Both your smell and taste receptors respond to chemical molecules dissolved in a liquid. In your nose the liquid is mucus; in your mouth it is saliva.

olfactory bulb

Odors enter.

palate

teeth

Food enters.

tongue

voice box (larynx)

taste centers

center for smell

SMELLING AND TASTING
Your smell receptors pick up odors and send signals to the center of smell in your cerebral cortex. The taste receptors on your tongue send signals to your brain's taste center.

tastes: bitter, sour, sweet, and salty. However, there are many variations and combinations of these.

Different parts of your tongue are sensitive to different tastes. The back of the tongue responds especially to bitter tastes, and the front and sides are sensitive to sweet tastes. As a person grows older, the number of taste buds may decrease, as does their sensitivity. This decrease can cut down on the enjoyment of eating, and so some elderly people have poor appetites.

Sensory nerves transmit signals from the taste buds to the brain stem. Then the signals travel to the taste center of the cerebral cortex.

Much of what we call taste is really smell, as you may realize when your nose is blocked by a bad cold. Working together, your senses of smell and taste produce a system sensitive enough to identify thousands of differ-

ent foods — and to make eating a most enjoyable experience.

Other Jobs for Your Nose and Tongue

In addition to your sensory systems, other systems of your body are served by your nose and tongue. Your nose serves your respiratory system by warming, cleaning, and moistening the air you breathe. Your tongue serves your digestive system by mashing your food and moving it around to be chewed and swallowed.

Both your nose and tongue help you to speak. Your tongue shapes the sounds you make, especially the consonants. Your nasal cavity, together with other cavities in your head (the throat, mouth, and sinuses), amplifies the soft sounds coming through your vocal cords so that other people can hear them.

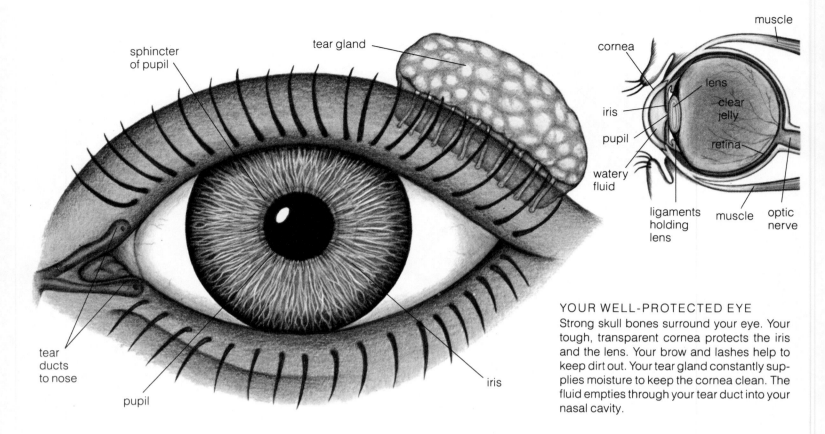

labels: muscle, tear gland, sphincter of pupil, cornea, lens, clear jelly, iris, pupil, retina, watery fluid, ligaments holding lens, muscle, optic nerve, tear ducts to nose, pupil, iris

YOUR WELL-PROTECTED EYE
Strong skull bones surround your eye. Your tough, transparent cornea protects the iris and the lens. Your brow and lashes help to keep dirt out. Your tear gland constantly supplies moisture to keep the cornea clean. The fluid empties through your tear duct into your nasal cavity.

Your Eyes

Of all the senses, eyesight is often considered the most important. Your eyes inform your brain about everything you look at. Through reading, your eyes bring you a wealth of information from other eyes and brains. According to one estimate, four fifths of everything we know reaches our brains through our eyes.

People often compare the eye to a camera. Both have lenses that bring images of objects into focus. Both have lens openings that can be adjusted to admit the proper amount of light. The eye transmits a constant stream of images to the brain by electrical signals — just as a television camera transmits images to your home screen. The eye, however, is far more sophisticated than any TV camera.

Information from Light Rays

Eyes receive information from light rays. Light rays travel from the sun or another light source to objects around you. The light rays are either absorbed or reflected. Objects that absorb all the light rays appear black, whereas those that reflect all the rays appear white. Colored objects absorb certain parts of the spectrum and reflect others.

When you look at something, the light rays reflected from the object pass through your transparent cornea.

Then your lens focuses the light rays on your retina, forming an image in reverse and upside down. From the retina, electrical signals transmit the image to your brain, which "sees" it as right side up.

The iris is the part of your eye — brown, blue, or some other color — surrounding your pupil. Looking through your pupil with a strong light, a doctor can see the blood vessels running across your retina.

Your lens is protected in front by fluid between it and the cornea. Behind the lens the eyeball is filled with a clear, jellylike substance. In a healthy young person, the muscles of the elastic lens can change its shape to bring objects at different distances into sharp focus on the retina. However, if the eyeball is shaped so that the retina is too near or too far from the lens, objects will appear out of focus.

When a doctor tests your eyesight, he or she may report the results in numbers that compare your eye with the normal eye:

$$\frac{20}{40}$$ means that your eye sees at 20 feet what the normal eye sees at 40 feet.

$$\frac{20}{20}$$ means normal vision.

$$\frac{20}{200}$$ means legal blindness.

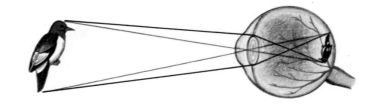

YOUR PUPIL ADMITS LIGHT RAYS

The pupil is the hole through the colored iris. Around the pupil is a sphincter muscle. When it contracts, your pupil gets smaller. Other muscles reach from the pupil to the outer rim of your iris. When they contract, your pupil enlarges.

YOUR LENS FOCUSES LIGHT RAYS

If you are looking at a nearby object, your lens thickens. If the object moves farther away, your lens thins out. This change of shape bends the light rays to keep the object in focus on your retina.

If your vision is out of focus, your own lenses can be assisted by other lenses: eyeglasses or contact lenses. Astigmatism is caused by an irregular shape of either the cornea or the lens. It can also be corrected with eyeglasses.

The retina lines the inside of your eyeball. In the retina are specialized receptor cells, called rods and cones, that contain light-sensitive chemicals. The rods (about 120 million in each eye) are used for black-and-white vision in dim light. The cones (about 7 million in each eye) function in full light and enable you to perceive colors.

Color blindness is due to defects of the cone cells. Different cones are sensitive to different colors, so that a color-blind person may be able to perceive some colors but not others. Color blindness is inherited and rarely occurs in women.

A newborn baby is naturally farsighted and cannot focus on nearby objects for several months. Young children usually have normal eyesight, but this may change as they grow.

Some older people may have trouble focusing on both near and far objects because their lenses have lost the natural elasticity. This problem can be corrected with bifocal lenses.

Tiny muscles control the movements of the eyeballs. The brain sends messages to these muscles, causing them to move both eyes in the same direction at once. When there is an imbalance in the strength of these muscles, a person may appear cross-eyed or walleyed.

Proper nutrition is important to preserve good eyesight. People who get too little vitamin A cannot see well at night. You get vitamin A in carrots and green, leafy vegetables.

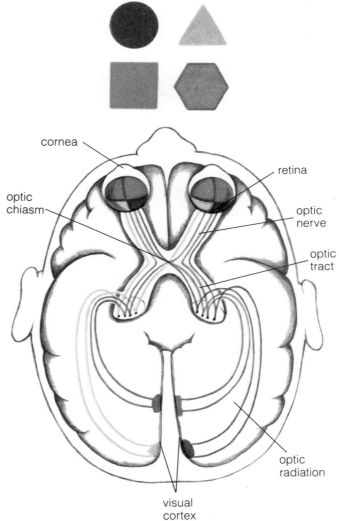

MESSAGES FROM EYE TO BRAIN

The visual information entering your eyes passes to the visual cortex at the back of your head. Your left eye and your right eye see the same object but from slightly different angles. Information from the right side of your left eye and from the right side of your right eye reaches the right side of your visual cortex. The information from your left eye crosses over in the optic chiasm.

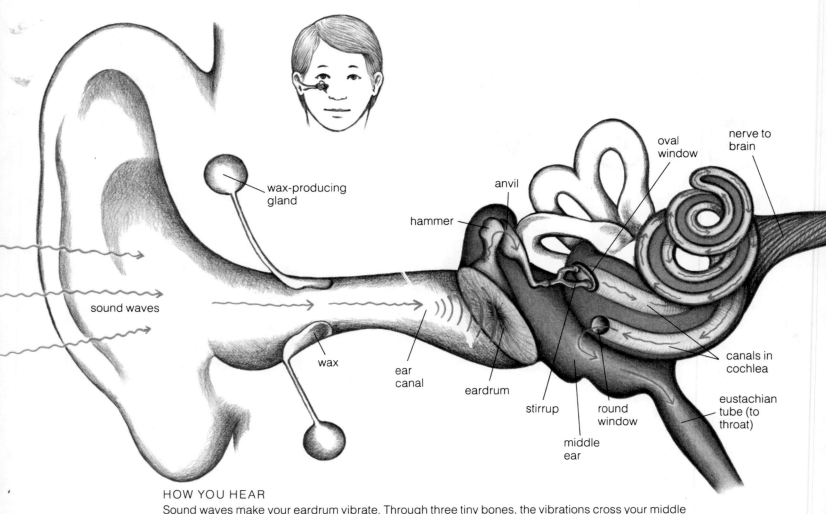

wax-producing gland

sound waves

wax

ear canal

eardrum

hammer

anvil

stirrup

oval window

nerve to brain

canals in cochlea

round window

eustachian tube (to throat)

middle ear

HOW YOU HEAR

Sound waves make your eardrum vibrate. Through three tiny bones, the vibrations cross your middle ear to the oval window, which leads to your inner ear. The vibrations pass into a coiled tube filled with fluid and lined with receptor cells. They convert the vibrations into electrical signals for your brain.

Your Ears

Your ears are not only organs of hearing but also organs of balance. They receive sound waves from the air around you, changing them into electrical signals that are "heard" by your brain. At the same time, your ears help you to stay upright.

Your outer ear collects sound waves and funnels them into the ear canal. The canal is protected by hairs and by wax produced in special glands. The hairs and wax trap dust and other particles, keeping them away from the eardrum. The eardrum is a thin sheet of skin at the end of the canal.

Your middle ear lies beyond the eardrum. Three tiny, delicate bones form a chain carrying sound vibrations from the eardrum across the middle ear. Because of their shapes, these bones are called the hammer, the anvil, and the stirrup. The base of the stirrup covers the oval window, a thin sheet of skin at the entrance of the inner ear. Since the oval window is much smaller than the eardrum, sounds become more concentrated as they cross the middle ear.

The middle ear is connected to the throat by a narrow tube, 1½ inches (4 centimeters) long: the eustachian tube. The tube normally is closed, but it opens automatically when you swallow or yawn. This helps to keep the pressure equal inside and outside your eardrum.

Inner Ear: Organ of Hearing

The inner ear is deep within your skull, behind and slightly below your eyeball. The receptor cells for hearing are in the cochlea. This organ is shaped like the shell of a snail. It is a fluid-filled tube coiled 2½ times around a central core of bone. Sound vibrations reach the tube through the oval window. Within the cochlea the vibrations in the fluid cause movements of tiny, hairlike nerve endings, 25,000 in each ear. The receptor cells convert the movements to electrical signals,

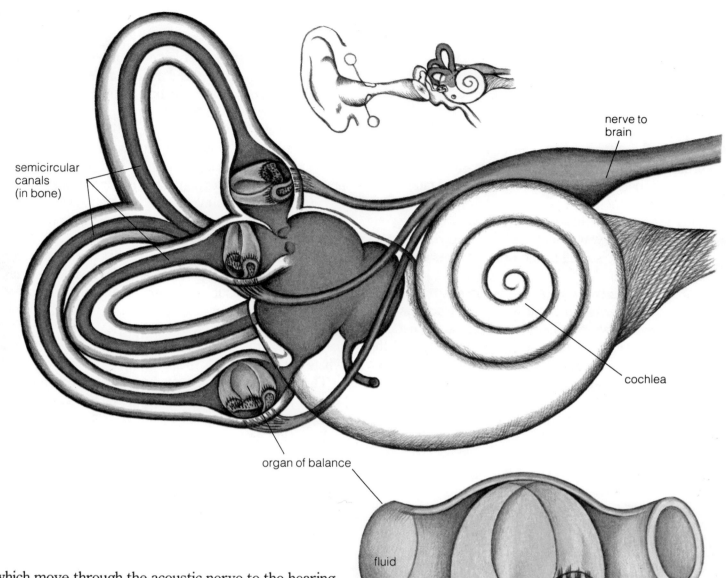

semicircular
canals
(in bone)

nerve to
brain

cochlea

organ of balance

which move through the acoustic nerve to the hearing centers of your brain.

Inner Ear: Organ of Balance

Next to the cochlea lies an organ that helps you to keep your balance. It contains three semicircular canals: one canal parallel to the ground, a second parallel to the side of your head, and a third parallel to your face. Receptor cells in the canals report to your cerebellum about the movements of your head.

When you spin around very fast, you feel dizzy for a few moments afterward because the fluid in the canals is still moving.

Other receptor cells are situated in and near the semicircular canals. As you bend or lean, tiny calcium crystals roll over the receptor cells. They report to your brain about your position in relation to the pull of gravity. Even if you swim under water with your eyes shut, you know which direction is up.

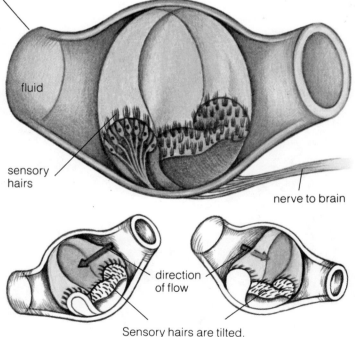

fluid

sensory
hairs

nerve to brain

direction
of flow

Sensory hairs are tilted.

HOW YOU FEEL MOVEMENTS OF YOUR HEAD
The three semicircular canals on each side of your head report its movements to your brain. Each fluid-filled canal contains an organ of balance with receptor cells. As you tilt your head, fluid presses on sensory hairs of the receptor cells. These cells convert the pressure into electrical signals for your brain.

Skin

YOUR SKIN IS the largest organ of your body. The skin of an average adult weighs 8 to 10 pounds and covers an area of about 22 square feet. Your skin grows faster than any other organ, and it keeps renewing itself throughout life. The skin is so important that a loss of more than one third of it from burns may be fatal.

The chief function of your skin is protection. It provides a tough, elastic, waterproof covering for your body. It protects you against harmful bacteria, temperature extremes, sunlight, and other threats from outside your body.

Your skin has two layers: the epidermis on the surface and the dermis underneath. The epidermis consists of several layers of cells. New cells are constantly being formed in the bottom layers and pushed up to the surface. At the surface, the cells accumulate a tough protein called keratin. Within a few weeks, they die and flake off.

Your thickest skin is on the palms of your hands and the soles of your feet. If you put more pressure on some of this skin — for example, if you play tennis — more keratin is formed. The resulting calluses provide extra protection for the tissue underneath.

Before birth, ridges and furrows form in your thickest skin. The patterns are different in each person, so fingerprints provide a useful means of identification.

Thin skin covers all your body surfaces except for the palms and soles. The skin over your eyelids is the thinnest of all.

Your epidermis also contains melanocytes, cells that produce a pigment called melanin. The amount of melanin in your skin determines the darkness of its color. Because sunlight stimulates the production of melanin, skin exposed to the sun darkens. Sometimes the melanocytes collect in clumps called freckles.

The bottom layer of skin, the dermis, is much thicker than the epidermis. It contains blood vessels, hair roots, glands, elastic fibers, and fat. Different nerve endings (sensory receptors) respond to touch, pressure, heat, and cold. Some of the nerves respond to pain, giving a warning that you must get away from whatever is causing the pain.

The sweat glands in your palms, soles, forehead, and armpits may respond to your emotions. For this reason, a nervous person may have moist palms.

Your skin also serves as a storehouse for fats and glycogen (the form in which your body stores glucose). It can absorb certain medicines applied to its surface. When your skin is stimulated by sunlight, it manufactures vitamin D.

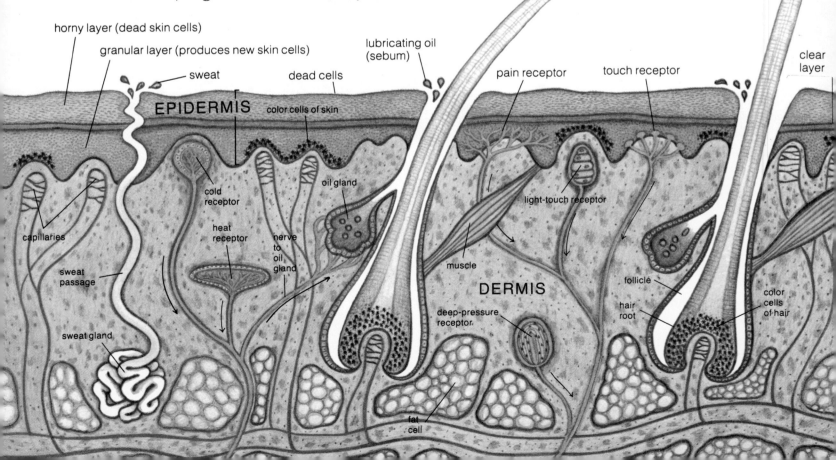

horny layer (dead skin cells)
granular layer (produces new skin cells)
sweat
dead cells
lubricating oil (sebum)
pain receptor
touch receptor
clear layer
EPIDERMIS
color cells of skin
cold receptor
oil gland
light-touch receptor
heat receptor
nerve to oil gland
capillaries
muscle
sweat passage
DERMIS
follicle
deep-pressure receptor
hair root
color cells of hair
sweat gland
fat cell

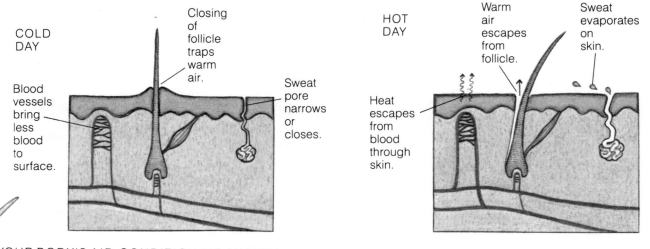

COLD DAY

Blood vessels bring less blood to surface.

Closing of follicle traps warm air.

Sweat pore narrows or closes.

HOT DAY

Heat escapes from blood through skin.

Warm air escapes from follicle.

Sweat evaporates on skin.

YOUR BODY'S AIR-CONDITIONING SYSTEM
Your skin and blood work together to keep your temperature steady. When your body temperature rises, glands in your skin produce sweat. At the skin surface the sweat evaporates, cooling you off. On a cold day, less blood flows near the surface than on a hot day.

Allergic rashes and hives can result from accumulations of tissue fluids in tiny spots within the dermis. The itching is produced by the irritation of nerve endings within the area. When enough fluid collects between the layers of skin cells, blisters form.

As people age, their skin changes. The dermis gradually loses some of its fatty and elastic tissues. The skin becomes thinner, drier, and more wrinkled.

Your Hair

Each hair grows from the bottom of a shaft, or follicle. Each follicle has a tiny muscle that contracts when it is stimulated by cold or by emotions such as fear. When the muscle contracts, it causes the hairs to "stand on end" and produce goose bumps.

The follicles also have glands that produce an oily material called sebum. Sebum lubricates the hair shaft and surrounding skin. At puberty, these glands may become overactive, producing too much oil. By clogging the skin pores, the oil helps to build up tiny pockets of dirt (blackheads) or infection (pimples).

The density of hair varies in different parts of the body. After puberty, sex hormones cause hair to grow in different places in men and women.

Eyelashes die and fall off after three to four months, whereas the hairs on the head live for three to four years. The hairs on your head grow about half an inch (1.3 centimeters) a month. Since only the base of a hair is alive, cutting the end has no effect on the rate of its growth. The color of your hair is determined by the amount of pigment and the number and size of tiny air spaces in the shaft of each hair. Through DNA you inherit the color of your hair, its tendency to curl, thickness, and maximum length. As a person grows older, the amount of pigment in the hairs may decrease, so that the color fades first to gray and then to white.

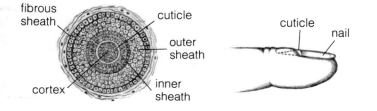

fibrous sheath

cuticle

outer sheath

cortex

inner sheath

cuticle

nail

Your hair and nails are specialized parts of your skin. They both contain the tough protein keratin, which also protects and waterproofs the outer layer of your skin.

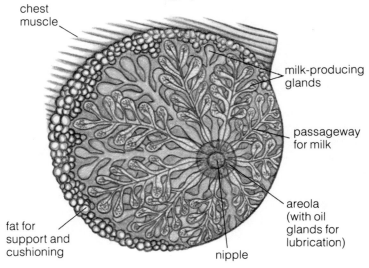

chest muscle

milk-producing glands

passageway for milk

fat for support and cushioning

nipple

areola (with oil glands for lubrication)

Both women and men have breasts, also known as mammary glands. Breasts are specialized sweat glands. After childbirth, a woman's breasts produce milk. Our mammary glands are what make us mammals.

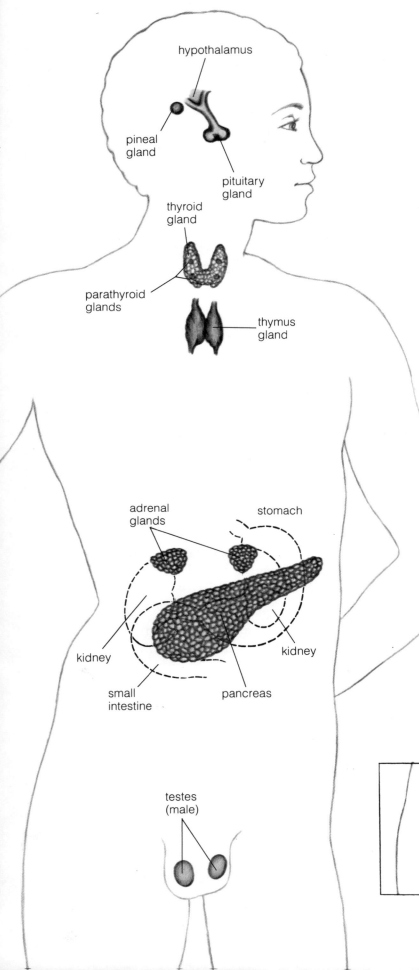

hypothalamus

pineal
gland

pituitary
gland

thyroid
gland

parathyroid
glands

thymus
gland

adrenal
glands

stomach

kidney

kidney

small
intestine

pancreas

testes
(male)

Endocrine System

ENDOCRINE GLANDS CONTROL many of your body's functions through chemical substances called hormones.

You have two kinds of glands. Your exocrine glands produce liquids such as sweat, saliva, mucus, and digestive juices. These reach nearby organs through channels, or ducts. Your endocrine glands, also known as ductless glands, pour their hormones into your bloodstream. Thus the hormones can reach distant parts of the body.

Some specialized organs have only one function: producing hormones. A few organs that produce hormones also have other functions. These organs include your stomach, small intestine, pancreas, and kidneys.

Control Center for Hormones

Your hypothalamus is at the center of the underside of your brain. It is connected to the rest of your brain and your spinal cord by many nerves. This organ serves as a link between your autonomic nervous system and your endocrine system.

The hypothalamus is responsible for many body functions. It has centers for the regulation of hunger, thirst, sleep, and wakefulness. It plays an important role in the regulation of most of the involuntary mechanisms of the body, including body temperature, sexual drive, and the female menstrual cycle. The hypothalamus also regulates the work of the pituitary gland.

The pituitary gland is sometimes called the master gland. Some of its hormones stimulate other endocrine glands to produce their own hormones. The pituitary, like the thermostat that controls the temperature of a building, has a feedback mechanism. Through this mechanism, the pituitary makes sure that enough of each hormone circulates in the body, but not too much.

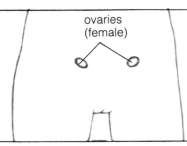

ovaries
(female)

YOUR ENDOCRINE GLANDS
While your nerves carry electrical instructions to specific muscles, your endocrine glands pour chemical instructions into your bloodstream to be carried to distant cells in your body.

Special Tasks for Hormones

The pituitary also produces hormones that go directly to the tissues that need them. One of the pituitary hormones regulates the retention of water by your kidneys. Another causes the uterus to contract during childbirth, and then stimulates the production of milk in the breasts.

One of the most important pituitary hormones is growth hormone. This controls growth by regulating the amount of nutrients taken into cells. The results of pituitary disorders may be dramatic. The smallest adult dwarf known was only 23 inches high and weighed 9 pounds. The tallest giant known grew to a height of 8 feet 11 inches and weighed 439 pounds.

Growth hormone also works with insulin to control the level of your blood sugar. Insulin is a hormone produced by your pancreas. If not enough insulin is produced, the blood sugar will rise to a very high level after a meal. This condition, diabetes mellitus, is the commonest disorder of the endocrine system.

The thyroid gland produces a hormone that affects the growth rate and metabolism of all your body cells. Under the surface of the thyroid gland are the four parathyroid glands. They produce a hormone that regulates the levels of calcium and phosphorus in your blood and bones.

The thymus gland influences the activities of lymphocytes in the spleen and the lymph glands. In an infant, the thymus is large. It becomes much smaller as a person matures.

Each adrenal gland consists of two glands, one inside the other. The inner part produces two hormones. When your sympathetic nervous system reacts to intense emotions, such as fright or anger, large amounts of the hormones are released. This may cause a "fight or flight" reaction, in which the blood pressure rises, the pupils widen, and blood is shunted to the most vital organs and to the skeletal muscles. The heart is also stimulated. This reaction is responsible for the extraordinary feats of strength that people sometimes perform in emergencies.

The outer part of the adrenal gland produces hormones that regulate the metabolism of carbohydrates, proteins, and fats. It also produces hormones that regulate the mineral and water balance of the body.

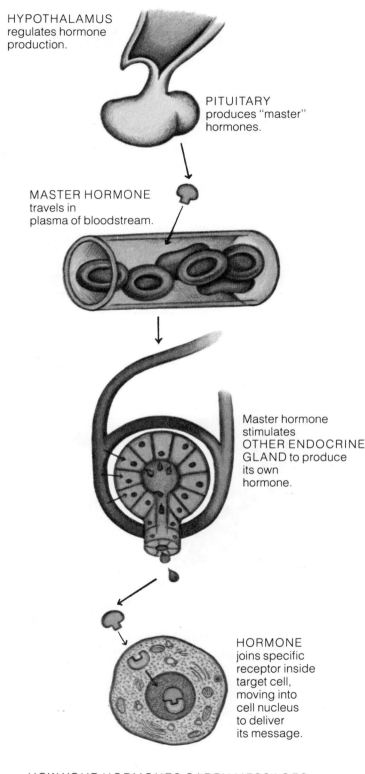

HYPOTHALAMUS regulates hormone production.

PITUITARY produces "master" hormones.

MASTER HORMONE travels in plasma of bloodstream.

Master hormone stimulates OTHER ENDOCRINE GLAND to produce its own hormone.

HORMONE joins specific receptor inside target cell, moving into cell nucleus to deliver its message.

HOW YOUR HORMONES CARRY MESSAGES
Acting as the master gland, the pituitary stimulates other endocrine glands to produce their own hormones for cells outside themselves. The pituitary also produces hormones to send directly to the cells.

Reproductive System

THE PURPOSE OF the reproductive system is the creation of a new human being. This happens when a sperm cell from a man fertilizes an egg cell from a woman.

The chief organs of the male reproductive system are the two testes (testicles) and the penis. The testes produce sperm, which the penis releases. Other parts of the male reproductive system help to store and to transport the sperm.

The Testes

The testes are egg-shaped glands, about 1½ to 2 inches (4 to 5 centimeters) long. They are contained in the scrotum, a bag hanging behind the penis out-side the pelvis. The scrotum consists of a layer of smooth muscle tissue covered with wrinkled skin.

Before birth, the testes are formed in the abdomen, below the kidneys. As the embryo grows, the testes travel downward, and by the time of birth they have usually reached the scrotum. Sometimes it takes one or both testes months or even years longer to reach the proper place.

The scrotum keeps the testes at the temperature necessary for the production of sperm. This temperature is slightly below that of the interior of the body. When the surroundings are too cold, the muscles of the scrotum contract, pulling the testes up toward the warmer abdomen. When the temperature becomes too hot, the same muscles relax, and the scrotum drops down slightly.

The testes contain endocrine cells, many tiny tub-

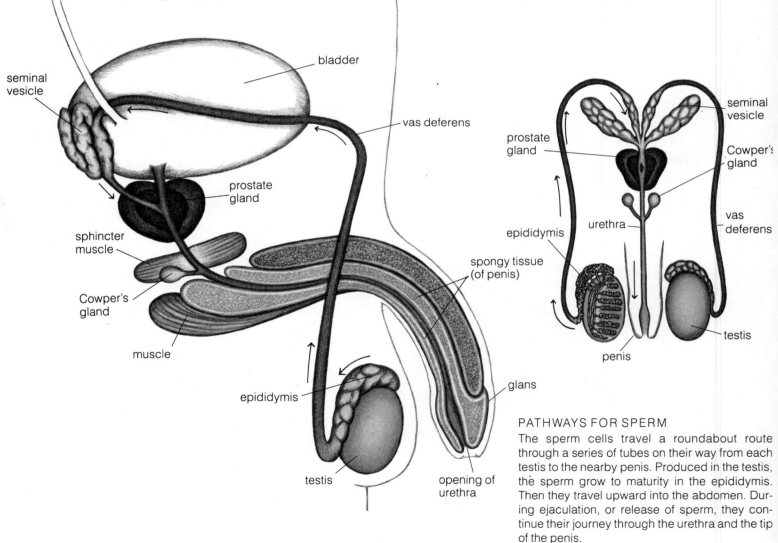

bladder

seminal
vesicle

vas deferens

prostate
gland

sphincter
muscle

Cowper's
gland

muscle

epididymis

testis

spongy tissue
(of penis)

glans

opening of
urethra

seminal
vesicle

prostate
gland

Cowper's
gland

urethra

epididymis

vas
deferens

testis

penis

PATHWAYS FOR SPERM

The sperm cells travel a roundabout route through a series of tubes on their way from each testis to the nearby penis. Produced in the testis, the sperm grow to maturity in the epididymis. Then they travel upward into the abdomen. During ejaculation, or release of sperm, they continue their journey through the urethra and the tip of the penis.

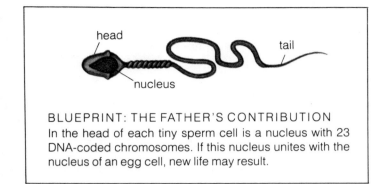

ules, and connective tissue. The endocrine cells are instructed by the pituitary gland to produce male hormones.

Testosterone, the most important of these hormones, causes the development of adult male sexual characteristics. These include the growth of hair on the face, chest, armpits, and genital area. At puberty, more of this hormone is produced. Testosterone is also responsible for increased bone growth and greater muscle strength. Growth of the voice box (larynx) results in longer vocal cords and a deeper voice. Later the same hormone may cause balding.

Each testis contains up to a thousand tiny, tightly coiled tubules. If uncoiled, each tubule would be as long as 38 inches (96 centimeters).

The tubules, originally solid, develop canals at puberty. The tubule walls are lined with cells that can develop into sperm cells (spermatozoa), the male sex cells. The production of sperm takes about six weeks. Sperm develop through a special form of cell division (meiosis) in which the number of chromosomes is halved. In human beings, the usual 46 chromosomes are reduced to 23.

Newly formed sperm constantly pass from the tubules to the epididymis. This is a thin tube, about 20 feet (6 meters) long and tightly coiled. Here the sperm are stored for 10 to 20 days while they finish growing. The mature sperm is approximately 1/500 inch (1/20 millimeter) in length.

Other Male Reproductive Organs

During sexual arousal, the mature sperm move from the epididymis to the urethra. Along the way, fluids from the prostate gland, the seminal vesicles, and Cowper's gland are added to the sperm. These fluids are able to neutralize the acids of both the male urethra and the female vagina, which would otherwise kill the sperm. They also provide nutrients for the sperm.

The mixture of fluids and sperm is called semen. Sperm can live in the male reproductive tract for several weeks, although they will die within two to three days after being released from the body.

The urethra is a tube running from the bottom of the bladder to the tip of the penis. During sexual arousal, muscles close the outlet from the bladder so that the urethra carries only semen.

The penis has three parts: the root, the shaft, and the glans. The root is attached to the pelvic bone. The shaft is made of masses of spongelike erectile tissue, which can fill with blood. The shaft is covered with loose skin.

The glans is the tip of the penis, where the slitlike opening of the urethra is found. The glans is covered by a free fold of skin (foreskin), which may be removed by circumcision.

Releasing Sperm

During sexual arousal, the autonomic nervous system causes a rapid flow of blood from arteries into the cavities in the spongy erectile tissue. At the same time, the veins contract, so that the blood is trapped in the penis. As the erectile tissue becomes stiff, the penis lengthens and broadens so that it becomes larger than usual.

Ejaculation, or release of semen, is caused by contraction of the involuntary muscles around the prostate gland, seminal vesicles, epididymis, and vas deferens. The semen may contain hundreds of millions of sperm.

Because ejaculation is chiefly under the control of the autonomic nervous system, it is, to a large extent, involuntary. During sleep, erections normally occur. An ejaculation during sleep is called a wet dream.

The Sperm and Reproduction

The head of each sperm contains DNA-coded instructions: half of the blueprint that will be transmitted to the baby if the sperm fertilizes an egg cell. By lashing their whiplike tails from side to side, the sperm are able to swim along the female reproductive tract. This journey takes the sperm about two hours.

Millions of sperm will die along the way. However, if only one sperm manages to meet an egg, fertilization may take place.

The Female Reproductive System

During each menstrual cycle, the female reproductive system produces a mature egg cell. If the egg is fertilized by a sperm, the mother's body protects and nourishes it while it grows into a baby ready to be born.

The chief organs of the female reproductive system are the two ovaries and the uterus. The ovaries produce one mature egg about every 28 days. The uterus provides the "nest" where a fertilized egg grows and develops into a baby.

The female reproductive system also includes three passageways. Two of them, the fallopian tubes, connect the ovaries with the uterus. The third is the vagina, which passes from the uterus to the outside. The vagina is where the penis releases sperm from the male's body during sexual intercourse. It is also the passageway through which a baby is born.

The Ovaries

The two ovaries are almond-shaped organs, one on each side of the uterus. They are quite small until puberty, when they grow to between 1 and 2 inches (2½ to 5 centimeters) in length. Girls usually reach puberty at about the age of 13, but there is wide (and normal) variation in the age.

Ovaries are made of immature egg cells surrounded by hormone-producing cells and connective tissue. A girl is born with 40,000 to 300,000 immature egg cells in each ovary.

Beginning at puberty, the ovaries produce one mature egg at the midpoint of each menstrual cycle. Since a woman will menstruate for 30 to 40 years, only a few hundred of her thousands of immature eggs will reach maturity. At menopause, the ovaries will shrink and will stop releasing eggs.

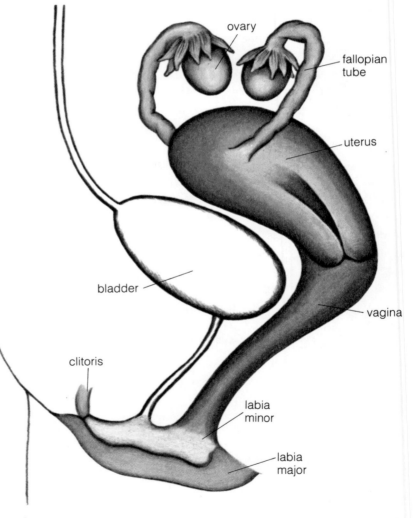

PATHWAYS FOR THE EGG CELL
Beginning at puberty, the ovaries release one mature egg cell about every 28 days. The egg is picked up by a fallopian tube, where it may be fertilized by a sperm. If the egg develops into a baby, it is nourished for nine months in the uterus. The baby is born through the vagina. If the egg is not fertilized, it is expelled through the vagina with the menstrual discharge.

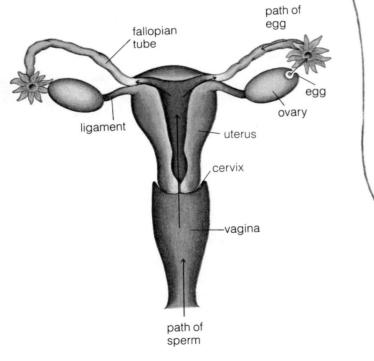

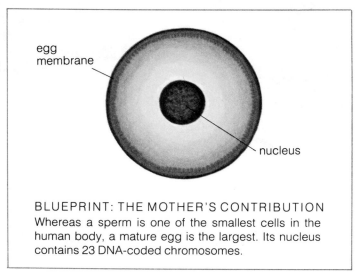

egg
membrane

nucleus

BLUEPRINT: THE MOTHER'S CONTRIBUTION
Whereas a sperm is one of the smallest cells in the human body, a mature egg is the largest. Its nucleus contains 23 DNA-coded chromosomes.

The Female Sex Hormones

Hormones from the pituitary gland regulate the work of the ovaries: the formation of mature eggs and the production of female sex hormones. These hormones, progesterone and estrogens, play important parts in the menstrual cycle and in pregnancy.

Estrogens are also responsible for the female sexual characteristics that develop during puberty. These developments include enlargement of the breasts, growth of hair in the armpits and the genital area, widening of the pelvis, and development of fatty tissue in the thighs and buttocks.

Producing Mature Eggs

An egg and its surrounding bubble of epithelial cells are known as a follicle. At the beginning of the menstrual cycle, in response to a pituitary hormone, several follicles move to the surface of the ovary. One of the follicles breaks open and releases the egg. This process is known as ovulation.

As a follicle matures, the fringed, trumpet-shaped end of one fallopian tube moves toward it. The fallopian tube may thus pick up the egg soon after the follicle pops open.

The empty follicle forms a small endocrine gland called the corpus luteum. This produces progesterone, which, together with estrogens, stimulates a thickening of the lining of the uterus.

The fallopian tube is lined with hairlike cilia. Their motions, aided by peristalsis of the tube walls, move the egg along the length of the tube. It is 4 to 5 inches (10 to 13 centimeters) long. Fertilization of the egg is most likely to occur near the beginning of the journey through the tube.

The uterus is a hollow organ, about the size and shape of a pear, with thick walls of muscle tissue. During pregnancy, the uterus stretches to become about a foot (30 centimeters) long.

During the menstrual cycle, the inner part of the lining of the uterus, the endometrium, is first built up and then expelled. During pregnancy, however, progesterone maintains a thick endometrium to nourish the fertilized egg and to prevent menstruation from occurring.

Completing the Menstrual Cycle

Menstruation is the shedding of the endometrium. If fertilization of the egg does not take place, the corpus luteum shrivels and hormone levels drop. The muscles of the wall of the uterus contract, expelling the endometrium and sometimes causing menstrual "cramps." Over a period of about five days, the uterus expels the unfertilized egg, bits of endometrial tissue, and some tissue fluid. The raw inner surface of the uterus bleeds a little. Usually less than 3 ounces (90 milliliters) of blood is lost.

The menstrual discharge passes through the neck of the uterus, the cervix, into the vagina. The vagina lies in front of the rectum and behind the urethra. (In the female body, the urinary and reproductive openings are separate.)

The opening of the vagina is protected by two sets of skin folds, the labia. Where the inner labia meet in front, there is a small mass of erectile tissue called the clitoris.

During sexual arousal, the clitoris will swell much as the penis does. In young girls, the opening of the vagina is usually protected by a thin fold of skin, the hymen. This may be stretched or torn during the first sexual intercourse or earlier.

The entire menstrual cycle, from the ripening of an egg to its discharge, takes 28 days on the average, but wide variations in this schedule are quite common and quite normal.

Even before menstruation ends, the pituitary hormones are already causing another egg to start ripening within its follicle. The cycle begins again.

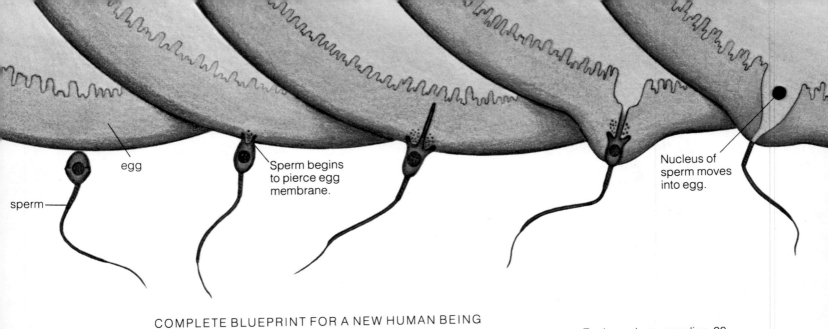

sperm

egg

Sperm begins to pierce egg membrane.

Nucleus of sperm moves into egg.

COMPLETE BLUEPRINT FOR A NEW HUMAN BEING
At fertilization, the nucleus of a sperm merges with the nucleus of an egg. Each nucleus supplies 23 chromosomes. The combined 46 chromosomes contain the entire DNA-coded blueprint for a new person.

New Life

The union of a female egg cell and a male sperm cell may result in a new human being. During sexual intercourse, semen released in the vagina contains 200 to 500 million sperm. If one sperm penetrates a mature egg, the membrane of the egg becomes impenetrable. Now no other sperm can enter.

Since each sperm and each egg have different sets of DNA, a great variety of characteristics are passed on from the mother and father. That is why brothers and sisters are alike in some ways but different in others. Sometimes two eggs are available for fertilization at the same time. If they are both fertilized, they will develop into nonidentical twins, as different as any other brothers and sisters.

In the fertilized egg, the 23 chromosomes from each parent line up and combine into pairs. One pair determines the sex of the baby. Sex chromosomes are of two types, X and Y. The egg contains only an X chromosome, but the sperm may contain either an X or a Y chromosome. If an X sperm meets an egg, an XX chromosomal pair will be formed and the baby will be a girl. If a Y sperm meets the egg, an XY pair will be formed and the baby will be a boy.

Fertilization usually takes place in the upper part of a fallopian tube. The newly fertilized egg begins cell division within 24 hours. If the egg splits into two separate parts on its way to the uterus, both parts may develop into babies. Because both have the same DNA-coded chromosomes in their cells, they will be identical twins.

NEW SYSTEMS FOR A NEW HUMAN BODY
The skeletal and nervous systems begin to form first, followed by the digestive and circulatory systems. By the time the fetus is an inch (2½ centimeters) long, almost all the organs of the human body have been formed.

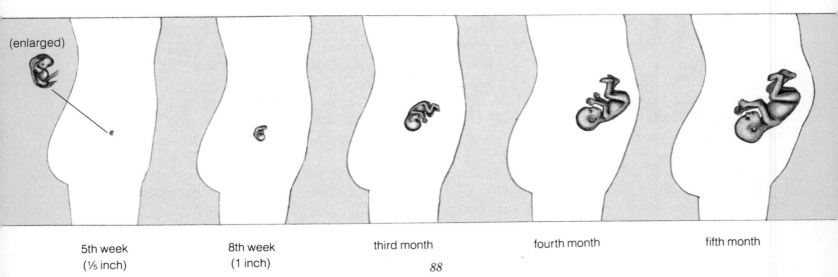

(enlarged)

5th week (⅕ inch)   8th week (1 inch)   third month   fourth month   fifth month

By the time the egg reaches the uterus, it has divided five or six times. Now it consists of 32 or 64 cells, clustered together like a hollow ball filled with fluid. Some of the outer cells reach out into the lining of the uterus to connect with blood vessels for nourishment.

This is the beginning of the development of the fetus's own special organ, the placenta, which has a thick network of blood vessels. The placenta serves as a barrier separating the fetus's blood from the mother's blood. However, nutrients and oxygen move from the mother's blood through the placenta to the fetus's blood so that it will grow. Wastes from the fetus move out through the placenta.

Before Birth

Within the first week in the uterus, three layers of cells form from the hollow ball. The various organs of the body develop from these layers. The outer layer produces the nervous system, skin, nails, hair, and tooth enamel. The middle layer produces the bones, muscles, kidneys, and circulatory system. The inner layer produces the respiratory and digestive systems and the glands.

As directed by the new DNA-coded blueprint, the number of cells rises from the single cell of the fertilized egg to the 6 trillion cells of the newborn baby. The cells develop into different tissues for their specialized work, but every cell (except the sperm and egg cells) contains the same complete set of DNA-coded instructions.

The fetus lives in a fluid-filled bag, the amniotic sac, which helps to protect it from injury. Within this sac, the fetus begins to exercise its newly formed body. During the earlier months of development the fetus is quite small, with a large amount of fluid around it. The fetus kicks its legs and swims around within the amniotic sac.

The fetus also experiences sensations. It can hear the noises of its mother's body. It can tell light from darkness. It can feel its own body and explore its environment with its hands. It sucks its thumb and swallows amniotic fluid. Before birth all the major body systems are completely developed.

The Birth of a Baby

When pregnancy is completed, a pituitary hormone stimulates the muscles of the uterus. They begin to contract to push the baby out. The opening of the cervix, usually only the size of a pinpoint, enlarges to let the baby through. The amniotic sac breaks, releasing a gush of amniotic fluid. A baby is usually born head first. With a cry, it takes its first breath of air.

Following the birth of the baby, the placenta separates from the wall of the uterus. It is pushed out by contractions of the muscles of the uterus. The pituitary gland releases other hormones that stimulate the production of breast milk in the mother.

The newborn baby is now ready to start life outside the mother's body.

GROWING TOWARD BIRTH
During the final six months of pregnancy, the fetus increases more than 100 times in weight and about 20 inches (50 centimeters) in length. At birth, the baby's body contains trillions of cells.

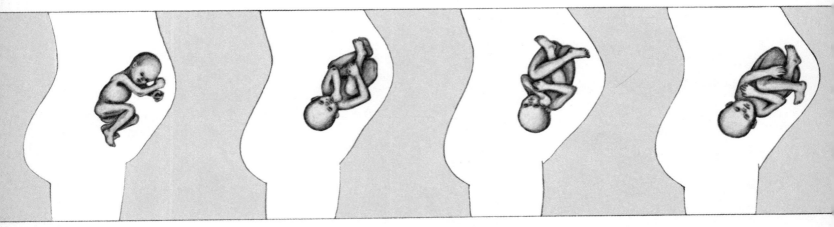

sixth month   seventh month   eighth month   ninth month

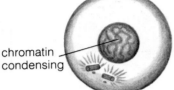

nucleus
(with
chromatin)

nuclear
membrane

centrioles

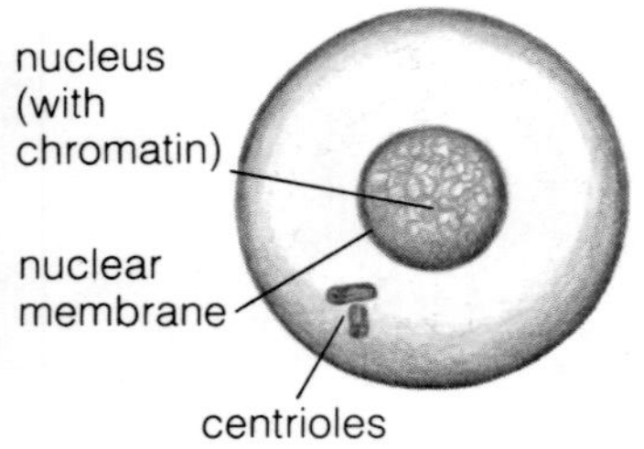

HOW YOUR BODY MAKES NEW CELLS (MITOSIS)

Before a cell divides, its nucleus contains chromatin (consisting chiefly of DNA). The cell's two centrioles are close together.

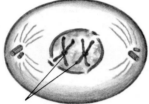

chromatin
condensing

The chromatin begins to condense into 46 strands called chromosomes. The centrioles start to move to opposite sides of the cell. Spindle fibers begin to develop around them.

chromosomes

Each of the chromosomes doubles into a pair of identical chromosomes. The membrane of the nucleus begins to break up and disappear. The contents of the nucleus mix with the cytoplasm. The centrioles reach opposite sides of the cell.

chromosome
(just before
dividing)

spindle
fibers

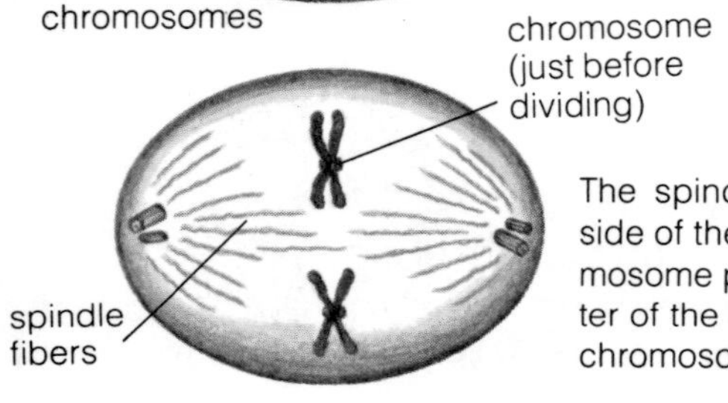

The spindle fibers stretch from one side of the cell to the other. The chromosome pairs line up across the center of the spindle. (Only two of the 46 chromosomes are shown here.)

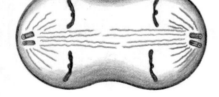

The two halves of each chromosome pair separate and move to opposite sides of the cell.

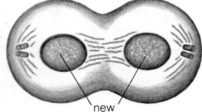

new
nuclei

Two new nuclear membranes develop. The chromosomes turn back into chromatin. The cell develops a "waist."

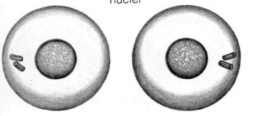

The two new cells are complete—identical in every respect to the parent cell and to each other.

Why Cells Divide

A human body contains trillions of living cells. Like every living thing, a cell grows and dies. Nerve cells, which cannot be replaced, last for most of a human lifetime. Other types of cells wear out after years or months. Red blood cells last for three to four months, but some white blood cells wear out in a few days. In the outer layer of skin and the inner lining of the digestive tract, cells last for a week or so.

During their lifetime, cells use raw materials from outside themselves to build up the substances they need for their survival and for their specialized work. They also break down stored nutrients to produce energy for their activities. All the physical and chemical changes that take place within the living cell — all the building up and breaking down — together are known as metabolism.

When cells mature enough, they reproduce themselves by dividing. Every minute, millions of cells in a human body die. Healthy cells keep dividing to replace them. So the number of cells in the body remains much the same throughout adult life.

The orderly process of cell division usually takes one to two hours. Cancer cells divide in a wild and uncontrolled manner, producing tumors.

In the usual process of cell division, mitosis, two identical new cells are formed from one parent cell. Both old and new cells contain 46 chromosomes. The sex cells, the sperm and egg, divide by a special process called meiosis. Each sex cell has 23 chromosomes. When the sperm and egg unite, the fertilized egg will have the normal number of 46 chromosomes, half from the mother and half from the father.

How DNA Works

In the nucleus of each cell are many thousands of genes. Genes instruct your body to produce all the molecules it needs, such as proteins. Although each cell nucleus has a complete set of genes, each cell uses only the instructions it needs for its own work.

Genes are made of deoxyribonucleic acid, or DNA. DNA is a long, thin molecule, best imagined as a twisted ladder. The rungs are made of four chemicals called bases: adenine (A), thymine (T), guanine (G), and cytosine (C). One rung consists of two bases, each attached to one side of the ladder. The base T matches only with A, and G matches only with C.

DNA has two important functions. First, it stores in the genes the genetic information inherited from the parents. Second, DNA directs the making of exact copies of itself.

To transfer the information in a gene, part of its DNA untwists and splits down the middle, as if the ladder were sawed in half. Another molecule called messenger RNA is made, using one half of the split DNA as a pattern. If the split DNA reads G-C-T, the messenger RNA will form C-G-A. Then the messenger RNA moves out of the nucleus to deliver its information to ribosomes in the cytoplasm of the cell.

In the ribosomes, proteins are made according to the orders brought by the messenger RNA. A protein chain is assembled from amino acids. Amino acids are brought to the cell for storage after they are broken down from proteins in food. Each type of amino acid is identified by a certain sequence of three bases.

The messenger RNA moves through the ribosome, three bases at a time. Each sequence of bases is recognized by molecules called transfer RNA. Obeying the sequence in the orders, molecules of transfer RNA come to the ribosome, each bringing its own amino acid.

As the messenger RNA moves along, the amino acids begin to link together like beads on a necklace to form a protein chain. Messenger RNA also instructs the ribosomes when to start assembling amino acids and when to stop.

When a cell divides, the DNA ladders in the genes untwist and split down the middle. With the help of a special protein, each half serves as the blueprint to make a copy of the other half. In this way two identical chromosomes are formed from one chromosome. And when the cell splits into two new cells, each has a complete set of DNA-coded instructions.

Your Own Special DNA

Each person has a unique genetic sequence. Your own special DNA controls your sex, height, color of eyes and hair and skin, immunity to diseases, allergies, and many other characteristics. Your DNA makes you different from everyone else in the world (unless you have an identical twin).

Your special DNA also directs the development, growth, and functioning of all the systems of your body, from the skeletal system to the reproductive system.

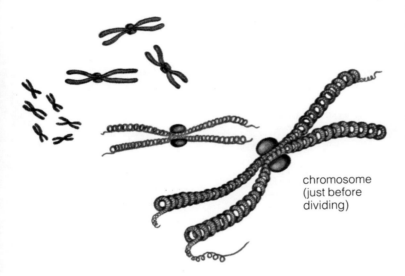

chromosome (just before dividing)

DUPLICATE CHROMOSOMES
Just before a cell divides, each chromosome doubles into a pair of identical chromosomes. One chromosome of each pair will move into one of the two new cells.

protein coating

DNA molecule

YOUR OWN DNA-CODED BLUEPRINT
DNA is the complex molecule that, with its protein cover, makes up a chromosome. It is shaped like a twisting ladder. The "rungs" carry a chemical code directing the formation of proteins. Every cell nucleus in your body (except the nuclei of eggs and sperm) contains a complete set of the DNA-coded blueprint you inherited from your parents.

INDEX

Page numbers in *italic type* refer to material in illustrations and captions.

sphincter muscles, 40, *43, 50*
  of anus, 40, *43, 47*
  of bladder, 43, *43, 66*, 67, *84*
  of eye, *43, 76*
  of stomach, *47, 48*, 49, *49*
spinal canal, *36*, 71
spinal cord, *13, 16, 18, 19*, 32,
    36, *68*, 69, *70*, 71, *71*,
    72, *73*, 82
  meninges of, 71, *71*, 72
spinal discs, *14*, 29, 36, *36, 71*
  slipped, 36
spinal nerves, *16*, 71, *71*
spine (spinal column, back-
    bone), *13, 18–19*, 32,
    36, *36*, 40, 71
  vertebrae of, *11, 13, 14, 16,
    18*, 32, *32, 33*, 36, *36*
  See also spinal cord
spleen, *13, 14*, 63, 65, *65*, 83
sprain, 37
starches, 45, *46*
sternomastoid, *11, 38, 39*
sternum. *See* breastbone
stirrup, 78, *78*
stomach, *13, 14*, 42, *44*, 45, *47,
    48*, 48–49, *49*, 82
stroke, 62, 63, 72
sugars, 45, *46*, 50. *See also*
    glucose; glycogen
sunlight, *43*, 80
superior vena cava, *19, 58*, 60
swallowing, 48, *54*, 56, *56*, 75,
    78
sweat glands, 28, 80, *81*, 82
synapses, 70, *70*

T

tail bone (coccyx), *32, 33, 36, 68*

tarsals (ankle bones). *See*
    ankles
taste, 72, 74–75, *75*
tear ducts, *10, 11*, 56, *76*
teeth, *10*, 45, *45–46*, 89
temperature, *43*, 45, 56, 58,
    60, 63, 69, 72, 80, *81*,
    82, 84
temporalis, *11, 38*
tendons, *21, 23, 24*, 29, 40, *41*
teres major, *19, 39*
testes (testicles), *16*, 35, *82,
    84*, 84–85
testosterone. *See* hormones
thalamus, *73*
thighbone, *14, 16, 22, 23*, 32,
    32, 33, 87
thirst, 82
thoracic nerves, *68*
thorax. *See* chest cavity
throat. *See* pharynx
thumb, *24*, 37
thymus gland, *13*, 65, *65, 82*,
    83
thyroid gland, *10, 13*, 35, *82*,
    83
tibia. *See* shinbone
tissues, *26, 28*, 28–29, *29. See
    also* connective tissue;
    epithelial tissue; mus-
    cular system; nervous
    system
toes, *24, 25*, 32
tongue, *11*, 45, *46*, 74–75, *75*
tonsils, *11*, 57, 65, *65*
touch, 71, *71*, 72, 74, 80, *80*
trachea (windpipe), *10, 11, 13*,
    48, *52, 54–55, 56*,
    56–57

trapezius, *11, 19, 38, 39*
triceps, *21, 38, 39, 41*
tuberculosis, 57
tumor, 90
twins, 88, 91

U

ulcer, 49
ulna, *21, 24, 32, 33, 37, 41*
ureters, *14, 16*, 43, *66*, 67
urethra, *14, 16*, 43, *66*, 67, *84*,
    85
urinary system, *14, 16, 26, 27*,
    39, 43, *66*, 67, *67*, 85,
    87. *See also* bladder
uterus, *14*, 43, 86, *86*, 87, 88,
    89

V

vacuole, *31*
vagina, *14*, 85, 86, *86*, 87, 88
valves, 60, *60*, 61
vas deferens, *16, 84*, 85
vegetables (in diet), 43, *46*, 51,
    63, 77
veins, *23, 25*, 60, *60*, 62, *62*, 65,
    65
  basilic, *21, 24*
  brachial, *58*
  cephalic, *24*
  coronary, *60*
  in exchange of gases, *58*
  femoral, *23, 58*
  inferior vena cava, *14, 19,
    58, 60, 66*
  jugular, *10, 13, 58*
  pulmonary, 60, *60*
  superior vena cava, *19, 58*,
    60

in urinary system, *66*
  See also blood vessels
ventricles, 60, *60*, 61
venule, *51*
vertebrae, *11, 13, 14, 16, 18*,
    32, *32, 33*, 34, 36, *36*
  and spinal canal, *36*, 71
  and spinal discs, *14*, 29, 36,
    36, 71
  See also spine
villi, 51, *51*
viruses, 57, 64, *66*, 71
visual cortex, 77
vitamins, *44*, 45, *47*, 51
  vitamin A, 45, 77
  vitamin D, 35, 45, 80
vocal cords, *54*, 75, 85
voice box (larynx), *10, 11, 54*,
    75, 85
vomiting, 48, 74

W

water, 28–29, 56, 83
  in cells, 30, 67
  and digestive system, *44*,
    45, *47*, 50, 51
  and urinary system, 67, *67*,
    83
wax (in ear), 78, *78*
white cells. *See* blood cells,
    white
windpipe. *See* trachea
wrists, *21, 24, 25, 33*